THE LOST SOUL

A novel by Diane R.J. Bibbins

DORRANCE
PUBLISHING CO
EST. 1920
PITTSBURGH, PENNSYLVANIA 15238

Dorrance Publishing Co
585 Alpha Drive
Suite 103
Pittsburgh, PA 15238
Visit our website at *www.dorrancebookstore.com*

ISBN: 978-1-6853-7230-9
eISBN: 978-1-6853-7769-4

DEDICATED TO

My father, John Johnson Sr. aka Dad, Daddy. A man of many great things was not just my dad, he was my mentor, best friend and most importantly my guardian angel. To this day I truly feel the presents of my dad walking by my side inspiring me as I continue my life's journey. That inspiration gives me strength to move forward in a positive way, and for that I'm thankful. Love you dad, always will. Rest in peace. June 20, 1928 – May 6, 1994.

My mother, Mae Alice Johnson, aka Sandi, Gurl-Gurl, Girlio. I am forever thankful that my mom's support gave me the confidence, strength, and faith, to always believe in the gift that God has given me. And I am truly grateful to my mom for keeping me on point when things seemed to be going in the wrong direction, by simply reminding me, "God has brought you too far to fail you now." I hold those words close to my heart. Mom, I will always love you. Rest in peace. December 13, 1933 – January 7, 2022.

Mom and Dad

IN LOVING MEMORY

John Johnson Sr., my father

Mae Alice Johnson, my mother

John Johnson Jr., my oldest brother

Henrietta Cropper, my grandmother

Shirley Dorothy Johnson, my aunt

They will always be in my heart

ACKNOWLEDGMENTS

I am eternally grateful to God for his presence in every step of my journey.

Denise Rivers Lynn – aka Dede, Little Dede Rivers I will forever love you, my sister. You taught me the meaning of friendship. You sheltered me when I felt homeless, you protected me when I felt vulnerable and for that, I say thank you. Your always in my heart!

Vernon Cole Webb – to my first love, I say thank you for making me feel loved. I will always be grateful that God afforded the two of us to take our journey together. Love you, my friend.

Shawn Warren – aka del Negro, my baby brother. My unwavering love for him is as strong today as the day he was born. He has always been an inspiration through my walks of life. He will always be my baby brother.

Allyson Johnson – aka Ally, my baby sister who I have always loved and admired. Ally, thank you for always being in my corner. My love for you will always be unconditional.

Karen Johnson Pilgrim - aka L&M, Pigeon, Underground, Sleepy, my younger sister who has always supported me through my endeavors. I will always cherish every step you have chosen to take with me. Our long night conversations about life are very important to me and I will hold each conversation we've had close to my heart. And for that, I say thank you. I am truly thankful for your untiring efforts working with me on marketing strategy. My love for you goes without saying. We make a great team! Love you Karen, always have, always will.

Michael Johnson – aka Mike, my older brother. My love for you goes without saying, we are family, thanks to mom and dad. I have, and always will respect you as my older brother. I pray, every day that Jehovah guides the two of us to come together as brother and sister. Hopefully one day, we can find in our hearts to unite as one. Love you Mike, always will!

John Johnson Jr. – aka Butch, our eldest brother, July 23, 1954 – January 29, 2015,, may he rest in peace. As the oldest sibling he chose to take on the overwhelming responsibility to be the loudest cheer leader in support of each of our struggles, dreams, and goals at an early age. Butch was a beautiful soul, he had a heart larger than life, and he shared it with all his siblings. We all understand that God called on him to come home. I truly believe his heart and soul is with us all today. Your respect, understanding, steadfast support, selfless love, and concerns, are missed. Love and miss you Butch! We all do. God's speed.

Shirley Dorothy Johnson – aka Bright eyes. I will never be able to express my gratitude to an aunt that was more like a second mom. She took me under her wing and helped to guide me through my walks of life. I am truly blessed to have had the opportunity to walk in step with this beautiful woman. Her faith in me gave me the strength to never give up on life.

Ella Freeman – aka Kim, CSM, Sal, Suckie, Suckface, you have a heart of gold and you have never disappointed me. Kim, you are my strength and my rock. I thank God every day for our unconditional love, friendship, and respect we have for one another. Sal, you are truly a blessing in my life, love you.

Jackie Johnson – aka Agent 77. My everlasting affection for my favorite sister-in-law, who's love, and confidence in me, has been unwavering. Thank you for always believing in me. I thank Jehovah for every day you're in my life. Love you Jackie, always will.

Cynthia A. Williams – aka Tweet, Buddie. I believe in my heart, that our relationship will never be disrupted by bullshit. Thank you for being there for me as a professional and most importantly, a friend. Our friendship means a lot to me, and I plan to hold on to it. I love you like a sister. God speed Tweet! P.S. Give my Burger King bandit my love. Lol, peace.

James Richards – my favorite supervisor whom I admire as a professional and respect as a leader. I am so thankful that he as a professional helped me to grab hold of my potentials. His unrelenting persistence to make me write was a gift from God. Thank you for keeping me in step with my surroundings which helped me to grow as a professional. I am forever grateful. God bless you and your family.

Nancy Mann – A beautiful soul that I will always love, admire, and respect as a colleague for never leaving me behind. Your actions and positive attitude screamed, one team, one fight. Your confidence in me, gave me the strength to successfully move forward. I can never thank you enough. God bless you and your family.

Kristi L. Artis – aka Rabbit. Thank you for always believing in me. Your endless editing support and advice helped give me the courage to move forward with my manuscript. You'll always be in my heart.

Aretha Fuqua – aka Rere. This incredible woman stepped into my life with an open heart. My gratitude for her unwavering support as a professional, colleague, and most importantly, a friend. You will always be special to me. Love you Gurl!

It's a circle of deception with a group of people (family and friends) that say they love each other but are stabbing each other in the back. It gives us insight as to why, we cannot trust one another. The only one that you can always depend on (trust) is yourself. That's my humble opinion.

You live only once, and you die when you can't help it…
The words of a wise woman!

Henrietta Cropper
(My grandmother)

PROLOGUE

"Jesus! What just happened?" she howled. She was discombobulated; nothing made sense. Shaking and crying overwhelmingly, she managed to pull over to the shoulder of the road, dropped her head onto the steering wheel as she wondered if he were dead. She had to defend herself; he was trying to rape her! One minute the two were sitting on the couch going over the case files and the next, he's all over her. One hand covering her mouth, and the other up her dress yanking at her thong. With her heart racing and her eyes bulged she managed to grab an artifact from the coffee table and hit him in the head until he was no longer moving. She wasn't sure how she made it out of there. The thought made her throw up.

She knew this business trip was a mistake, it was last minute and not well planned. However, this was her chance to get a break away from her alcoholic mother and overprotective father. She agreed to second chair; after all, she was familiar with the case. With that, she agreed to fill in for the colleague that was initially scheduled to make the trip. That didn't matter now, she could be facing murder. She blurted, "I need to get home, Dad and Uncle John will know what to do." She decided she had no choice but to drive all night. She got herself together, spun off merging into traffic.

Tycie Spaulding was traveling north on I-95 in her red Mercedes-Benz E 350 convertible, with the top down. It was a beautiful night with a warm breeze. The sky was clear and there was a full moon. Tycie was an attractive single woman in her thirties. She had a beautiful caramel complexion with light-brown eyes, long black hair, and beautiful white teeth. Her posture was perfect. When she walked, she walked with confidence and grace. When in public, she always came across as full of life and she was a damn good lawyer working on a partnership despite her uncertainties.

She was thankful to be back in Kentucky. She had been driving for hours. It was a beautiful morning, and she was almost home. Tycie decided to take the next exit to get gas and stretch her legs. As she exited, she noticed a park off from a distance and decided to head that way after she got gas. She needed to gather herself before facing her father. As she drove through the park, she spotted a bench near a set of monkey bars and decided to park. Tycie parked her car, got out, walked over to the park bench, and sat down. She wasn't tired, just depressed. As she sat there looking into the distance, she observed a strange-looking man standing alongside a tree. She couldn't make out his facial features, but she could see that he had long blond hair under a Yankees baseball cap. He had on jeans with holes in both knees, a jean jacket, and what looked to be old work boots.

She looked away when she felt he noticed her staring at him. Several minutes later she looked his way again and noticed a woman with a slight limp hobbling toward him. She was a slim woman with pale skin and short black hair. The two were almost dressed alike except for the Yankees baseball cap and work boots he was wearing. He extended his arms as she approached, and the two embraced. *I wouldn't be surprised if they were having an affair*, she thought, shook her head, and muttered, "People!" in disgust.

She took a deep breath, leaned back, and rested her head on the back of the park bench, then closed her eyes.

As Tycie relaxed enjoying the warm breeze blowing across her face, she thought of her grandmother. She enjoyed the long conversations the two of them shared on Sundays. It was during those conversations she came to realize what a wise woman her grandmother was. She thought of one of the last things her grandmother shared with her not long ago. *"You live only once, and you die when you can't help it."* That thought brought tears to her eyes. She couldn't help it; it was him or her, she thought. As a few minutes passed, she got lost in her thoughts and drifted off.

The figure loomed yelling, "Hey!" at the top of her lungs. Tycie's eyes snapped open. The sun was somewhat blinding. There was an image between her and the sun. She raised her hand to block the sun to make out the dark figure. As she attempted to focus, she made out the figure to be a bony-faced woman with a birdlike nose. The woman had something in her hand pointing it in her direction. When she started to speak, the woman sprayed something in her eyes that made them feel as though they were on fire. She wailed, clutching her eyes with one hand and flapping the other in the air.

As she awkwardly tried to stand yelling at the top of her lungs, "YOU BITCH!" two large hands transfixed her from behind, snatched her over the back of the bench, threw her to the ground, and hit her in the back of the head with a large hard object. The world as she knew it, went black.

Tycie's eyes opened slowly, still irritated as she rapidly blinked. She was discombobulated, not knowing how long she has plummeted into unconsciousness. Tycie's body and head were killing her. As she struggled to figure out where she was, she touched the back of her head, it felt moist and warm. When she tried to look down at her hand it was too dark for her to see anything. She was cold and started shaking uncontrollably. She tried as hard as she could to figure out where she was. Her mind drew a blank. This didn't make any sense to her.

As she struggled to get up, her head hit something and she couldn't move any further, she felt closed in. Several seconds later she heard horns blowing and felt a slight motion. As the thought registered, she attempted to yell, "Oh my God…, I'm in the trunk of a car," but nothing came out.

Chapter 1

HAS YOUR LIFE BROUGHT HAPPINESS TO OTHERS

Selina Sander's aka Terri was a very unhappy little girl. She was fair-skinned, leggy, with a button nose and French braids. She lived with her mother, aunt, and uncle. Selina was the only child in the house. There were times, she found herself wondering why her aunt Penny treated her more like a daughter than her mother, Angela.

Selina spent most of her young life under the impression that Angela was her older sister. It was almost as if the two of them were casual acquaintances. They had nothing in common and communicated only when necessary. Angela's treatment toward Selina was mean, cruel, rude, disrespectful, and shameful.

Selina would cry herself to sleep most nights because she didn't understand what it was that made her mother treat her so terribly. For as far back as Selina could recall, living under the same roof with Angela was a challenge. The two never spent any time in the same space; when the child walked into a room, Angela would walk out. She never showed her any type of affection; it was almost as if she hated her. As time went on, things between the two of them, only worsened.

On Selina's thirteenth birthday, Aunt Penny sat her down, looked her in her bright eyes, and shared with her who her birth mother was. The news was so shocking, the child stiffened, her eyes filled with tears, and she couldn't speak. Aunt Penny gently cupped Selina's face with her small hands and whispered in her ear, "Angela may be your birth mother, but you'll always be my baby girl."

Selina wailed, "Who is my father?"

Aunt Penny whispered ever so softly, "You've had enough for one birthday." With that, the two embraced and just sat there without another word.

That evening Aunt Penny felt troubled. She had not been totally honest with the child. She could not find it in her heart to tell Selina who her father was. She didn't feel the child could handle it under the circumstances. Aunt Penny realized the two were on this destructive journey alone.

Aunt Penny had forgiven Jeff for his disgraceful act with her sister. Penny gave what love and concern she had left to care for Selina; she was the innocent one in all this mess. *Jeff is raping this child; what do I do?* she thought. This child cannot survive in this environment. As Aunt Penny sat on the side of her bed, she started crying and shaking uncontrollably. The thought made her sick to her stomach. How can Jeff rape his own daughter?

Selina was afraid to say anything about the continuation of assaults. Aunt Penny was sure Jeff was raping the child and she's known for several years.

That one afternoon, Penny was on her way to the Piggly Wiggly to pick up a few items. One and a half blocks away from home, she realized she'd forgotten the grocery list. As Aunt Penny entered the house, she heard the child crying and Jeff saying, "Shut the fuck up. If you say anything about this, I'll put you out on the street like a lost dog and nobody can do anything about it. You stay here because I let you. This is my house!" he yelled. "I pay the bills here; you only eat because I let you. I didn't hear you say thank you Uncle Jeff for letting me stay here." The child's bottom lip was trembling as she said in between sobs, "Thank you, Uncle Jeff."

"Now take your ass upstairs and clean yourself up before Penny returns," Jeff said with malice in his voice.

Tears rolled down Penny's cheeks as she slowly backed out of the house without saying a word. She ran down the street breathing heavily, crying and confused. Her mind raced. *Did that just happen?* she asked herself. *Oh my God, again, not again. She's only a child.*

Chapter 2

HAPPINESS IS NOT A WET PIECE OF ASS AND A CIGARETTE IN THE MORNING

Angela spent most of her time at the tavern around the corner from the house. Tall, high yellow, full-figure, well-spoken, and bowlegged, Angela Sanders was always well dressed; nothing was ever out of place. When Angela sashayed down the street, heads would turn. She was a very proud proper young woman, who felt the world owed her something. She was very flirtatious, which made it a special pleasure for most men to be in her presence.

The evening slowly developed into much of nothing. It was the usual crowd with a few new faces, but nothing of special interest. With another wasted night under her skirt, she decided to go home. *Yeah home. Nah, fuck that, it's my sister's home. This shit was almost a joke,* she thought. She'd planned to move out the first chance she got, and she knew the only way that plan would go full circle would be to get married. *A girl's got a do, what a girl's got to do,* she thought. As she sashayed around the corner, back to her temporary "home."

As Angela approached the front door and turn the knob; it didn't budge. Shit, it was locked. It was only 11:30 p.m., and the agreement between her and Penny was midnight on the front door. She stood there for several seconds trying to decide if she should ring the bell or check the back door. She decided on the latter.

As Angela approached the backyard there stood her fine-ass brother-in-law. That muscular frame standing at the back door smoking a cigarette with the light from the kitchen confirming he was shirtless. Jeff was a high-yellow brother with hazel eyes, curly black hair, and juicy red lips. She was sure he was drunk as usual.

"Good evening, Jeff. Kinda late for you to still be up, ain't it?" No response. This was his house, which was the main fucking problem. She asked, "Where is Penny?"

"Her ass is in bed where yours should be," he replied. From his tone, she knew he was getting ready to start his bullshit rant. "Your ass thinks just because you got a light complexion you can stay out half the night! white boys don't hang out at that hole around the corner," he said.

"Jeff, why do you say that?" she said.

He shouted, "Shut the fuck-up!" As usual, his breath reeked of alcohol, but it was something about his demeanor tonight that aroused her. She slowly moved closer toward him; she could feel his hazel eyes watching her. As she stepped within inches of his handsome face, their eyes locked, she noticed his wet plum lips slightly separated as his tongue slowly wiped across his bottom lip.

She blindly stepped into his mouth and their tongues touched, his hot breath and warm tongue melted her in his arms. He placed the palms of his hands firmly on her ass and pulled her closer. She felt his erection as he pulled her into him. He had her ass firmly in the palms of his hands. As they stumbled backward into the kitchen, she heard him mutter ever-so-softly in her ear, "Shit" as they fell to the floor. It was almost as if it were in slow motion.

He rolled ever so gently on top of her. *Oh. He still has an erection*, she thought. They looked into one another's eyes as he slowly rubbed his rock-hard erection against her sex. She could feel her vagina pulsating as he whispered in her ear, "Please." He raised her skirt and slowly started removing her undergarment. She wiggled her hips left to right to help him get them off. When the cool air hit her sex, she realized just how wet her pussy was. He slowly slid his finger into her vagina. As he slowly moved his finger in and out of her personal space, her thighs uncontrollably trembled. As her head slowly dropped back, and her back arched, she begged Jeff to put his business inside of her.

Jeff took his time kissing and gently sucking her neck. As he slowly moved his tongue between her cleavage, he slid his warm juicy tongue toward the tip of her right nipple. He slowly sucked her hard nipple as if he were a newborn baby being breastfed. As he nibbled on her nipple, she couldn't wait any longer. Her nipples were so hard, and her sex was so wet. She pleaded for more. As he looked her in the eyes, he unzipped his pants, pulled out his rock-solid penis, grabbed her hand, and cupped it inside of his, and placed it around his penis. She was shocked to feel how large and hard it felt. He guided her hand as she slowly stroked his penis. His breathing became heavy as he guided her hand toward her vagina. As he started penetrating her with his hard rock, she cringed, and a tear trickled down her cheek. His thrusts were deeper and harder as he moved faster and faster. As he stiffened, her eyes closed, and she bit her bottom lip not sure if she felt pain or pleasure. One thing for sure, her brother-in-law's business was done.

He didn't use protection...

Chapter 3
KEEP ME SAFE, KEEP ME SAFE

She woke up from a deep sleep feeling nauseous another morning. At first, she didn't understand what was going on, by day five she figured it out. After she took her face out of the toilet, it convinced her it was time to confide in her sister Penny. Confused and afraid, she had no choice; her options at a minimum equaled zero.

Penny would know.

At 7:00 a.m. on what seemed like a beautiful spring morning, and she hadn't slept a wink. She looked out her bedroom window into the blue sky, scared and confused. She's carrying her brother-in-law's child. Why did she let this happen? How does she tell her sister she slept with her husband? Angela dropped to her knees trembling and began to pray.

She shared her morning problem with her sister Penny. A thin, homely looking woman with a hunchback, high cheekbones, and dead dark eyes. She came across as timid; however, her strong presence took control of the room. She was a very polite soft-spoken woman.

Her reaction to the baby news was interesting. She mumbled several words with her eyes closed. Then she asked, "Girl, have you been sleeping around?"

Not sure how to respond, a few seconds passed as she cleared her throat and shouted, "You mean having sex?"

Sister Penny replied, "I knew you were up to no good hanging at that tavern like some cheap floozy." As Angela started to speak, guilt forced her to her knees, she grabbed her stomach, dropped her head, and wailed, rocking back and forth frantically, "It's Jeff's."

"Jesus!" Penny muttered.

Nine months later, it was a baby girl.

Chapter 4

WHAT WE HAVE IS HARD TO COME BY

It was a difficult birth. Angela thought she would die during labor. She promised herself this sin would never happen again. As the large Black nurse was rolling her back to her bed, she boomed, "It was a baby girl. You should be proud she has five little fingers on each hand, five little toes on each foot and she looks like she might get by. Folks today hope to have children with a bright complexion and the right number of things. You should be thankful," she said with a broad smile from ear to ear. Angela didn't understand why the beefy nurse was so overjoyed about this…what came out of her was a sin, a dirty sin.

She thought back to the evening she and Penny approached Jeff about their sin. Jeff refused to take responsibility when confronted. He told Penny he would never commit such an unforgivable act. "She's your sister for God's sake," he yelled with tears in his eyes. He couldn't explain why Angela would lie about something like this. Maybe she's trying to get somebody to take care of it, damn it. After they went back and forth, Penny decided she had heard enough.

She abruptly stood and said, "Fine, who gives a damn. The bottom line is Angela is pregnant and she's my little sister. We'll all do what we must do," and walked out of the room. Jeff jumped up in disgust and stormed out behind Penny, pleading for her to listen to him. Angela perplexed and shamed, her brother-in-law just lied to her sister. Who did Penny believe!

To avoid seeing her, Jeff would stay out most nights and Penny spent her time praying. That was the worst nine months of her life.

Angela lay there in a fetal position feeling sorry for herself. The hospital was releasing her today, and she was so unsure of her future. In her mind, God was punishing her for sleeping with her sister's husband. Angela refused to live under the same roof with that thing. It would remind her of the sin for the rest of her life.

She could not face that guilt from day-to-day. What was she going to do? She thought about the beefy nurse that went on and on about how happy she should be about her mistake. Angela's decision was made; it was the only way she would have a life. After all, it was all about her happiness.

Angela talked plenty to the large beefy Black nurse that came to her bed to change her I-V and gave her a dose of medication. The morning of her release. Beefy made her final trip to her bedside. Angela calmly said, "You know somebody that wants a baby?" Beefy stepped back in what seemed like slow motion with a look of astonishment on her face, bulge eyes, and mouth wide open.

She resounded, "Girl! Did you say you looking for givin' away your baby?"

Angela thought for a second and nervously blurted, "Yes!"

Beefy stared into Angela's warm brown eyes for several seconds and boomed, "I'll take her!" Beefy went on. "When I get off, I'll sit outside your area and wait for you to check out. Leave the baby in the cart in the far corner of the space." Angela agreed.

Sister Penny showed up at the hospital around 2:00 p.m. to check her younger sister out. As Penny approached her sister's room area, she noticed a large Black woman sitting outside of the area entranceway. Penny stepped in front of the beefy woman and asked, "Who are you?"

Beefy said, "I'm the one that girl in there promised her baby to."

Sister Penny studied the beefy woman for a few seconds and politely said, "No, madam, you're not taking that baby anywhere."

The beefy woman clumsily jumped to her fat feet, sticking out her oversized index finger and shouting at the top of her lungs, with spit flying all over the corridor, "Who do you think you are?"

Penny went into her purse, grabbed her bright white handkerchief, and slowly dabbed the splatter of spit off her face. With each gesture, there was a slight smile on her face. Penny went on. "Since I'm my sister's legal guardian, she has no say in this matter." Penny stood her ground long enough for the beefy "bitch" to respond with…nothing she could hear as she entered the open entranceway to her sister's area.

Penny walked to her sister's bedside, feeling shame and disgust. She muttered in a low tone, "Is this how you rid yourself of the sin? Are you that trifling?" No response. Penny knew she had done no wrong today at the hospital. She just claimed what belonged to her. After all, she knew who the father was! That became a reality they all had to live with, as the years went on.

Chapter 5

TWO BROTHERS WALKING THEIR DOG

Tom, Aaron, and their dog Lucky were walking along State Road 1311 in Garysburg, North Carolina, also known as the Jackson Bypass, when their dog Lucky took off running and barking into the woods. Aaron took off behind Lucky yelling, "Come here, boy, here, boy." Lucky kept running for a few more feet before he came to a sudden stop. Aaron noticed the dog clawing at something and pushing whatever it was, with his nose. As Aaron slowly approached, he wasn't sure what it was he was seeing, he snapped, "Come here, boy!" With a nervous tone.

Lucky stopped, instantly turned away from whatever it was, and with his tongue hanging out, he trotted toward Aaron panting.

As Aaron took several more steps forward to meet Lucky, his eyes widened as he fell to his knees, grabbing his stomach while vomiting. He quickly fell back on both hands, raised his buttocks, and did the crab walk in more of a running motion with both feet and hands moving as quickly as they could while yelling, "Oh my God" at the top of his lungs!

"Oh my God, Oh my God, Oh, My, God!" Aaron said over and over as Tom slid into his right side with both knees and grabbed him in his puny chest yelling at the same time, "What is it?" With his bottom lip trembling, Aaron muttered, "She's dead! Oh my God... she... she... she's dead," raising his right arm and pointing with his bony finger while trying to catch his breath, Aaron went on, "Oh my God, she's dead, Tom, dead," he muttered as though he were trying to prove his point.

Tom snatched his cell phone from its case, hit 9-1-1, and barked, "Please send help, a woman's been hurt bad, please hurry, she needs help!"

The operator said, "Sir, please! Calm down and tell me where you are?" Tom rattled off their location as best he could by flashing back to their location from the roadside before running into the woods. The operator repeated every word to Sergeant Patterson who responded with, "Car 24 in the area, on my way, over!"

The battered woman was flown by helicopter to John Randolph Medical Center in critical condition. This nude, beaten, bloody body was found in the woods facedown. The woman had been beaten, raped, sodomized, strangled, and left for dead. *Who is she, who did these unspeakable acts?* Sergeant Patterson wondered.

Sergeant Patterson taped off the area as a crime scene.

Chapter 6

A LOVE THAT COULD NEVER LIVE BUT WILL NEVER DIE

Ty was at the house out back practicing his jump shot when his cell phone rang. He pulled it out of his jacket pocket after making his jump shot and looked at the caller ID before answering, he mumbled, "Shit, now what?" He simply answered, "Ty!"

Terri yelled at the top of her lungs, "Our daughter is missing, you son of a bitch! What are you going to do about it?"

"What do you mean Tycie's missing?" Ty snapped.

She kept yelling as though he'd said nothing. "She hasn't been to work in several days, and none of her friends have heard from her since the day before yesterday. This is so unlike her; she is more responsible than this." He took a deep breath and asked her to calm the fuck down. She was going on and on about nothing that seemed to matter to him. His concern was his daughter, but he was somewhat confused at what Terri was trying to say because she was talking fast and yelling at the top of her lungs. He tried as hard as he could to put what she was saying into perspective.

He sat down in the middle of his basketball court and grabbed his forehead. It took all he had to be cool. *It shouldn't be this hard,* he thought. He reminded himself that their separation was because of her heavy drinking. He tried as hard as he could to accept their current situation out of respect for their daughter. However, it was times like this that made him wonder, how he fell so in love with this woman so many years ago. *This woman is a stranger to me now,* he thought. *Who is she?* he wondered. *When, why, and where did we go so wrong?* That thought took Ty back to their past. The past was all he had left to help him remember how much he did love her. As Terri went on and on, Ty's thoughts drifted elsewhere. He thought back to their younger years; they were so happy. He remembered the day they met.

Chapter 7

SHE NEVER SAW HIM COMING

Selina noticed the time; the library was about to close. She wasn't ready to go home, so she decided to take the trolley downtown to the theater. She wasn't sure what was playing, but it didn't matter, she wasn't ready to go home.

Imitation of Life was going to start in twenty minutes. She decided to get a pop before going in to be seated. She'd been in line about three minutes when she realized she had to use the john. There were only two people in front of her and she was too close to the checkout counter to get out of line. If she got out of line now, no way would she be seated before the show started. There was only one toilet for colored folks and that line was just as long. Two more minutes passed, and the line seemed to be at a standstill. She didn't want to miss any of the show.

She realized she was swaying from left to right when she bumped into this fine brother walking by. He stumbled ever so slightly to the right, catching his feet and throwing his left hand toward Selina as he blurted, "Whoa!"

His handsome face turned her way. He had a beautiful smile. She noticed how straight and white his teeth were. "Oh…my goodness, I'm so sorry," she said as they looked into each other's eyes. He noticed how beautiful she was as they

19

faced one another. Still smiling he quickly replied, somewhat loudly, "No, you don't have anything to be sorry for, I wasn't watching where I was going. Are you okay?"

Selina just stared into his eyes as she struggled to answer his question. "Ye-yes."

He replied, "Good, this isn't the kind of thing I do to meet good-looking women." He smiled warmly and told her to enjoy the show. Before she could reply, he was gone.

She decided against the pop and went to the john.

Chapter 8
HITTING THE SWEETEST NOTES

The show was great, she enjoyed it. She was sure Aunt Penny would love the movie; it was a tearjerker. Lora Meredith a single mother and an ambitious actress takes in a homeless Black widow Annie Johnson and her daughter that she meets at Coney Island. They lived in a small one-bedroom apartment and their struggles were real. One woman prioritizes her career and neglects her daughter and the other does all she can to get her daughter's love. Annie's little girl Sarah was the worse, she refused to accept she was Black. The light-skinned daughter rejects her mother's love and tries to pass as white whenever in public. Sarah's mother was embarrassing and hindering her. The racial bias made her angry and she did whatever she had to do to pass as white.

Aunt Penny has always said you have to love yourself before you can love someone else. Annie dies heartbroken, her daughter was ashamed of her, just because she was Black. The daughter barely made it in time for the funeral service, crying and asking for her mother's forgiveness. Her actions were disgraceful and too damn late. That thought made Selina think about her pathetic relationship with her mother.

It was late, and she wasn't in the mood right now for that long trolley ride back home. Just as she stepped outside, the trolley was passing her corner. She attempted to run and quickly changed her mind as she watched the rear of the trolley disappear. She decided to walk over to Main Street to Mack's convenience store to have a pop while waiting for the next trolley.

As Selina walked through the door of Mack's convenience store, there he was with his fine ass. He was talking with another guy. Selina sat several stools down from them. Mack walked over and asked, "How can I help you, miss?"

Selina replied, "Large birch beer, please."

Mack replied, "Coming right up!"

That handsome young man turned her way. When he realized it was Selina, he smiled from ear to ear. When she returned the smile, he got up and walked over to her and extended his hand as he was saying, "My name is Tyrone, my friends call me Ty."

She took his hand and said, "My name is Selina and my friends call me Terri."

He replied, "Is this seat taken?"

Selina answered, "No, please." When he sat down, she looked into his dark-brown eyes and smiled. He was a very handsome slim young man. She loved his bronze complexion, strong facial features, high cheekbones, slim lips, broad shoulders, and jet-black curly hair. As they looked into each other's eyes, he crossed his arms and put them up on the counter as the two of them sat there smiling from ear to ear as they enjoyed one another's conversation while sipping on a pop, without a care in the world. Five years later, they were married. Two years after that, they had a beautiful baby girl. That thought was interrupted when he thought about his mom and three siblings. They never met his daughter or ex-wife. He lost his immediate family so many years ago.

That took him back to his childhood, it was a period of his life that he would never forget...

Chapter 9

PEOPLE CARE ABOUT PEOPLE WHO CARE ABOUT THEMSELVES

Mrs. Spaulding was a sweet woman with a heart larger than life, and to him, she was his whole world. Tyrone was the oldest of three other brothers, Anthony, Matthew, and Andrew. When they were separated, he found it hard to stop looking back. His life wasn't the same without his mom and three brothers. Tyrone would spend the rest of his young life trying to understand why they were separated.

Mrs. Spaulding was a fair-skinned petite Afro-American Black woman with a bony handsome face, high cheekbones, green eyes, slim lips, and a headful of long black beautiful hair. She was a very strong Black woman that overcame many struggles throughout her life. Mrs. Spaulding was a kind woman with a heart of gold. With her quick wit and positive attitude, it was always a pleasure to be in her presence. Her kindness helped her and the boys survive over the years.

Mr. Spaulding walked out on Mrs. Spaulding and the boys years ago. She was raising her four young sons alone. Her oldest son was the head of the house. He took on more responsibility than most adults. She could depend on Tyrone; he never disappointed her. Tyrone loved his mom almost as much as he loved life. Tyrone didn't understand why, or how his father could just walk away from the family. Tyrone vowed to be a better man.

As time went on, Mrs. Spaulding's health dwindled, which made taking care of her four sons more difficult. It was 1936, the economy was weak, depression lingered, and tornadoes touched down throughout the United States as never before. During the spring of that year, Mrs. Spaulding died a painful death of bone cancer.

Tyrone did his best to take care of himself and his three brothers. She hadn't prepared the boys for this. As time went on, it became increasingly harder for the boys to get by. That winter Tyrone's three younger brothers were taken away, they became wards of the state. The thought of being separated had never crossed any of their minds. The three brothers were placed in the same foster home. The Smiths didn't mind taking in the three younger brothers, but they felt Tyrone would be more of a problem because of his age.

As the oldest, Tyrone knew going with the Smith's would be the best thing for his brothers. As they parted, Tyrone wondered if he'd ever see them again.

President Roosevelt was reelected to a second term.

Chapter 10

SHUT UP, SHUT UP, SHUT UP

Now years later, Ty was sitting in the middle of his basketball court listening to his ex-wife yelling at the top of her lungs, telling him his only child was missing.

He finally said in a nervous whisper, "Please calm down, Terri." She shut up and wept! He repeated what he thought he understood her to say. Terri forced herself to say no, in between sobs as she continued to cry.

She blurted, "You have to find our daughter, oh my God something bad has happened."

Terri pulled herself together and passed on what little information she had as calmly as she could. "Tycie departed North Carolina several days ago on her way back to Kentucky from a business trip. She decided to drive because she had planned to visit her close friend Gloria Kowalski in the Georgia area on her way back." Terri went on. "I've called Gloria several times and she has not seen or heard from Tycie in the last few days."

After Terri passed on the little information she had, Ty assured her everything would be all right and hung up.

Ty didn't understand why Tycie never mentioned this business trip to him. The two of them spoke about her birthday and made plans for dinner a little over a week ago.

He always thought they were close and shared just about everything as father and daughter. He had to be dreaming; surely his baby girl wasn't missing. She just needed some time to herself. *No! This isn't like her, she's too responsible and she knows how her mother worries,* he thought.

The longer Ty sat in the middle of his basketball court with his face in his hands, the more worried he became.

He snatched his cell phone from his jacket pocket and called his close friend JC Cole. JC and Ty have been friends for more than forty years. The two met in the military when they were stationed in the Netherlands as military police in the Army. JC was the best man at his wedding, and he was Tycie's godfather. He was like family. *Sharing this information with him is not going to be easy; he loves Tycie as much as Terri and me,* Ty thought.

JC was a tall broad-shouldered distinguished-looking man. With his lentil complexion, hazel eyes, and salt and pepper hair, the women loved him. For his size, he was very soft-spoken, but his arrogance made a strong statement. He has been divorced three times and had three sons that he helped conceive during each marriage. He loved his sons, all three of them, but he didn't see them as often as he'd like. They were between three different states, and he didn't have visitation rights because of his work. He almost lost his third spouse when she was kidnapped and held for ransom. That period of his life still weighed heavily on his heart. The kidnapper was another FBI agent from within. He no longer had respect for the FBI because of the amount of involvement within the organization with his wife's kidnapping. That whole situation made him feel there was a black cloud over his head. No longer enjoying being part of that team anymore, he retired. He decided to go into business for himself as a private investigator.

His social life now involved an attractive defense attorney named Rae Wyatt in a law firm with two other partners, Jones and Peters. Rae understood that marriage was not something that the two would ever speak of. They were just as happy as any married couple and they both loved Tycie. She was like a daughter to Rae as well.

"Yo, Ty!" JC boomed as he answered the phone. "How's it going, buddy?"

Ty's response was slow and weak. "Hey, JC, need to talk," he replied.

JC dropped his feet off his desk onto the floor and sat straight up in his chair while saying, "Ty, is something wrong, my brother?"

Ty took a deep breath and calmly said, "John, Tycie is missing."

"What did you say! Tycie is missing. What in the fuck do you mean missing?" JC replied.

"Yes, missing, I just got off of the phone with Terri, and she's a nervous wreck," Ty replied.

"Where are you?" JC asked.

Ty replied, "At the house."

"Stay there…I'm on my way!" he said as he jumped in his car and sped off.

Chapter 11

SHIT HAPPENS

When JC got behind the wheel of his Ferrari coupe, he floored it. Before he knew it, he was pulling into Ty's driveway. He left the engine running as he jumped out and ran into the house yelling for Ty.

When the two men were face-to-face, they did the usual buddy hug with a quick double pat on the back while shaking hands and a slight pause for assurance.

When JC stepped back, he said, "Talk to me, man! What's going on with our girl?"

Ty dropped his head, put his hands in his pockets as he walked over to his recliner, and dropped the weight of his limp body into the chair , glassy-eyed and his voice trembling as he whispered, "I don't know."

"What do you mean you don't know?" JC nervously questioned.

Ty pulled himself together and suggested to JC that he sit down. When he sat down, Ty shared the information that Terri shared with him. As JC listened, he realized Ty and Terri didn't know much about Tycie's disappearance. Neither had spoken with her in several days. That was a concern to him. JC jumped to his feet and said, "Let's go."

"Go where?" Ty asked.

"I'll tell you on the way," JC replied. When in the car, JC said, "We're going to Terri's. It would be best to have you both together to help one another recall Tycie's movements over the last couple of weeks.

"I didn't know she was going out of town for God's sake. We made plans for dinner for her birthday! That was over a week ago," Ty exclaimed.

"I understand that, but the two of you together can help one another recall her movements before the trip that you didn't know about."

Ty said, "Man, we have to find her. She's all I got."

JC replied, "Don't worry, I promise I'll find her, she means a lot to Rae and me also."

Ty said, "If anything has happened to her, I don't know what I'll do."

JC said, "Dude, don't think like that; she's okay. I will not work another case until I find our girl, I promise."

As they drove along, Ty blurted, "I hope this doesn't make Terri start drinking again; you know her and alcohol don't get along."

"What do you mean, man. We all drink!" JC said more like a statement than a question.

Ty took a deep breath, closed his eyes, and blurted out the family secret. "Several years ago, Tycie and I were at the movies when my cell vibrated. I got up from my seat as I was signaling to Tycie, give me a minute because I couldn't hear. I walked into the lobby and asked Terri to speak up. As she made the painful attempt to speak, her words slurred, so I could barely understand her. On the third attempt, she managed to slowly mutter in a barely, audible tone, 'Ty, please stay on the phone with me until I get home?' That shit came at me in slow motion, the bitch could barely talk! Man, I went the fuck off. 'Stay on the phone with you until you get home? Where are you? Stay where you are; my God, don't drive in your condition. Are you out of your fuckin mind?' The next thing I heard was a dial tone. I don't know why or how we were disconnected; I just knew I was, scared, worried, and confused."

"After the call was disconnected, I made a couple of attempts to reach Terri with no success. I didn't want to upset Tycie, so I decided to use the men's room, and afterward, I stood in line for another drink. Just as I started to place my order, my cell phone vibrated, it was Terri. I just walked away from the concession stand as I was yelling 'where in the fuck are you?' Terri managed to stammer, 'I'm in the garage.' I barked, 'In who's garage?' Terri slurred, 'In ours, silly. I'm home!' That whole thing just fucked me up. The last thing I remember about that call was yelling at the top of my lungs, 'Why in the hell would I stay on the fucking phone with your silly ass while you're driving drunk?' Before she could answer, I introduced her sorry ass to Mr. Click. She sent a half-ass text message that I didn't respond to because it didn't make sense. Later that evening I was at the house getting my shit together to move out, while Terri was passed the fuck out in her car in the damn garage. Two weeks after that she signed her crazy ass into rehab."

"Dude, wait, that's around the time you told me ole-girl was out of town on business."

"Yeah, right! It was business all right. That was the lie I decided to tell because I was disgusted and ashamed. Man, Terri lost her job a year before that bullshit happened: for drinking on the job."

"So, when you told me you moved out because you guys had grown apart, that was a lie?" JC questioned.

"Man, I don't know who this woman is anymore. Just a few weeks ago, Tycie and I both agreed that rehab had helped Terri. She was a much better person when she didn't drink. I can't stand to be around her when she's intoxicated. She feels sorry for herself, drives, lies, and can't remember shit when she's intoxicated. I couldn't do it anymore, I just couldn't."

"Alcoholics drain the ones they love. Not intentionally, however, it does happen, and it's sad. Being an alcoholic doesn't make you a bad person. It's the decisions you make after being told over and over , when sober, how bad you are when drunk, and you continue to drink! That should be an indication, you need help."

"Yo! Brother, crank it down. That is your daughter's mother."

"Just because I chose to share my nightmare doesn't give you the right to join in," Ty said.

JC jumped back in quickly with, "I'm just saying—"

"Not now, man, let's move past this. Let's just keep this simple. I'm just trying to bring you up to speed on the perfect Spaulding family," Ty said. "To this day, Terri, Tycie, nor I have ever mentioned that night. Tycie and I have no idea where Terri was or how she managed to drive herself home in that state of mind."

After several seconds of silence, Ty continued, "Do you always drive this thing this fast?"

JC clipped off, "Yep, there isn't any other way to drive it! It was made for speed! You feel me?"

"I feel you!" Ty replied with a slight smile.

The two rode in silence the rest of the ten-minute drive to Terri's. One man praying to himself, *I hope she's not drunk when we get there*, and the other praying, *I hope I can find my best friend's daughter and my goddaughter unharmed*.

Chapter 12

'IN LIFE, EVERY DAY IS A MONEY-MAKING DAY

When Cracker Jack pulled into the driveway in the Mercedes-Benz, he pushed the button on the rearview mirror that opened the garage door. Stump looked over at him and said, "How can we be sure no one's home?"

Cracker Jack painted the picture with no remorse. "Trust, the bitch didn't lie! In between her answers to my questions, she was crying and pleading for her life. I threatened to stab her in her left eye as I was fucking her, holding her throat tighter and tighter, then she passed the fuck out! Which is why she couldn't give us directions! So, I realized her vehicle has GPS, I select home and the directions to the house populated. Simple, don't make me regret bringing your ass along."

"Why so over the top this time?" Stump questioned.

Cracker Jack said, "Don't get shit twisted, nobody cares what the fuck you think! Get that old shit off your mind; that's behind us. I need you to refocus, we've come too far for me to let you fuck this up."

"I'm not going to fuck up, Cracker Jack. I know how important this is to you. I just didn't think it would come to this."

"No, you don't know how important this is! Now shut the fuck up and get the fuck out. Let's get this shit done," he growled.

Cracker Jack and Stump entered the house through the inner garage door, which was unlocked as Tycie said. That entryway took them into the laundry area. Once through the door, a pleasant fragrance filled their nostrils. Stump said, "Wow, it smells good in here."

Cracker Jack said with clenched teeth. "Shit! Damn it."

Stump whispered, "I thought you said, nobody was home!" When he faced her, he grabbed her bony face and pulled her in close enough for her to smell his funky hot breath.

He spat in her face and told her to wake the fuck up! "This is not a dream; this shit is happening in real life. We can't be too careful, remember shit for brains, we're thieves! No situation is ever safe for us, you dig!" Before Stump could part her lips to answer, Cracker Jack punched her in the stomach so hard it made her gasp.

Before she realized what happened, he grabbed her by the throat hard enough to make her eyes bulge and her face turn beet-red. He pulled her in close as she gasped and whispered in her ear, "Lay your boney ass on the floor."

Cracker Jack helped Stump ease her fragile bony body to the floor. When he dropped his 200-pound body on top of her 110 bony body, she gasped for air as she tried to suppress her coughs. He looked down at her bony face and licked the slobber from his spit attack moments earlier. He looked her in her empty eyes, paused, for several seconds as his pipe thickened. He thought, *do we have time for this?* Stump felt his erection and put her arms around his neck and attempted to pull him closer as she was separating her thin lips. He bit down on her bottom lip, and she flinched as he raised his large body off her, he said in a raspy smoker's voice, "Not now. We don't have time for this shit." Stump closed her knock-knees and slowly got up off the floor in disgust.

Chapter 13

HOME RUN

Several hours later every room in the house had been ransacked by the odd couple. It didn't look like the same place. All the takeaway was placed on the floor of the sunporch. Two 65-inch flat screens, several paintings, two computers, four iPods, camcorder, digital frame, three digital cameras, jewelry, ten thousand in cash, etc. They were in hog heaven; this was turning into their biggest score of their lives.

Cracker Jack said, "I knew changing our gig would bring in more money."

Stump said, "Yeah, we don't just rob them anymore. You beat, rape, and do whatever else it is that you do to them."

Cracker Jack said, "I do what I have to do to make money. Experience has been my best teacher; you really should keep that in mind." Stump didn't respond to that, instead, she walked into the kitchen, opened the refrigerator, grabbed two beers, went back into the living room, handed Cracker Jack a beer, and said, "Now what?"

Seth was on the floor of his nasty van cold in a fetal position, shaking like a leaf on highway 65 north in a rest area when James Brown screamed, "Please, Please, Please," several times. Seth pushed the button and slowly said, "You got me!"

Cracker Jack snapped, "It's time, get the fuck up and come on. Lights out, around back, as we discussed."

Seth repeated, "As we discussed."

Cracker Jack said, "By the way, seats out?"

Seth said, "Out!" and hung up.

Cracker Jack said, "Seth's on his way."

Stump said, "Seth, who is Seth?"

"You don't need to know that. How did you think we'd get out of here with this shit?"

Stump said, "The Mercedes-Benz."

"The Mercedes-Benz? All this stuff can't fit into the Mercedes-Benz. By the way, genius, don't you think they'll be looking for her and the Mercedes-Benz! Damn it, I planned this. I can't per-ten to be stupid. Just do what I tell you." When she touched his hand, he snatched it away and said, "Let's just wait for Seth."

A vehicle slowly approached the house with the emergency flashers on. Cracker Jack flashed the flashlight once and the emergency flasher's cut off. The van backed in alongside the rear of the house, to the door of the sunporch.

As Cracker Jack trotted down the several steps, Seth jumped out of the van and the two greeted each other with a quick dat-a-boy hug. As they parted, Cracker Jack said, "Let's get this done."

Seth said, "That's what I'm here for. What we got!"

When Seth got to the top of the stairs, he saw this fragile frame off from a distance and said, "Who in the fuck is that?"

Stump said, "Fuck you!"

Cracker Jack said, "Don't worry about that; let's just get this done."

Seth rolled his eyes and said, "Yeah right, let's just do this."

As they loaded the van, Seth said, "Damn, man, how'd we get so lucky?"

Cracker Jack said, "None of your business; don't worry about that. Let's just get this done, goddammit!"

Seth sucked on the gap where his two front teeth use to be, rolled his eyes, and thought to himself, *Dude, how in the fuck did you get so lucky? What is your secret?*

After the van was loaded, Cracker Jack confirmed the next few steps of their plan with Seth. He emphasized dumping the car as he jumped behind the wheel of the van. "Give us five minutes before you pull out," Cracker Jack warned. Stump was in the back of the packed van sitting on the tire rim with both legs pressed against her breast-less chest. She was confused and tired. She closed her eyes and rested her head against the wall of the van. Ten seconds later, her eyes popped opened as she gestured and mumbled, "My backpack," then she paused and thought, *I can't tell Cracker Jack, oh my God, this crazy motherfucker will kill me if he finds out!*

Chapter 14

MOTHER NATURE

"We've been over and over this. It's been a long night. JC don't get me wrong; Terri and I appreciate you taking the time to help us. I just feel like this isn't getting us any closer to finding our girl."

"I understand, but this has helped," JC said.

"How?" Ty asked.

"We have somewhere to start. Terri said she was in Garysburg, North Carolina the last time they spoke."

Ty said. "And?"

"We have somewhere to start," JC replied.

An hour later they were both back in the Ferrari. JC had it wide open headed south on I-65. "We have to backtrack to find her. The best way to do that is to go where Terri heard from her last and work our way back toward home," JC said.

"Brother, I hope you're right because we don't have anything else to go on."

"Trust me, my brother, we'll find her," JC said. "Okay, copilot, tell the GPS where we're going so that it can get us there."

Ty replied, "Got it." Ty slapped the voice control and barked: "Destination 708 Old Highway Rd, Garysburg, North Carolina 27881." The GPS suggested a couple of options that broke down hours, minutes, and miles. They both agreed with the ten hours and thirty-five minutes. JC knew he could get them there in less time if he kept the siren screaming and lights flashing.

Ty said, "The number is 252-555-1212, shouldn't we give them a heads-up about our visit?"

"No, the best way to go about this is to catch them off guard. Oh, remember. I've retired from the FBI, throwing that around would do more harm than good, just follow my lead. I'll keep us legal and at the same time ask the right questions to get us answers."

"Got it, I'm cool, relax man, it's all good," Ty said.

They stopped a couple of times for gas, coffee, and personal relief. Both men were too unnerved to eat. They were just focused on getting where they were going and praying for the best. Both men withdrew into their own space. This was when the two were most comfortable with one another. The two men were deeply in thought. They both took advantage of the quiet time. This was serious, and only God knew how it was going to turn out. Both were going to do whatever they had to do legally to find Tycie.

They both had a lot on their minds. JC stayed focused on the road. He refused to accept a negative outcome. He knew he would bounce into whatever the situation called for when the time came. Right now, his main concern was getting there. Ty felt something wasn't right. *Too many unanswered questions*, he thought. Ty laid his head back on the headrest and closed his eyes. Several minutes later, he drifted off to sleep as he thought back to when they lived in Philadelphia, Pennsylvania where Tycie was born. He slept with a slight smile on his face.

Terri and Ty spend the start of March 1958 back and forth to the hospital. The first week had been false alarms. The third week developed into a bad winter storm. By day four, 3 feet of snow later, Terri yelled, "My water broke." Ty jumped right into action. He grabbed the keys to the car, sprinted to the front door, snatched it open, and stopped in his tracks. He saw nothing but snow as far as the eye could see. He froze in place with his mouth hanging open as his lips slowly mouthed, "Shit!" There was so much snow, he could only see the tops of the cars. Terri's yells quickly turned into sound bites of "do something, motherfucker! This shit is serious, God Damn it!" Ty ran into the kitchen and snatched the receiver of the phone up and dialed 9-1-1 as quickly as his fingers allowed.

Ty clipped off, "Please send an ambulance to 106 Summit Place, my wife is in labor."

The operator said, "Sir, have you seen how much fuckin' snow is out there?"

"Yes, that's why I'm fuckin' calling," Ty snapped back.

"Then you know damn well an ambulance is out of the question for at least several hours," the operator shot back. Terri was in the background pleading for Ty to do something, as she continued to call him motherfucker with the start of anything she blurted out.

Ty yelled, "I don't care if you send a goddamn fire truck, just send somebody" and slammed the phone down. When Ty ran into the bedroom Terri was laying across the bed, eyes blistering, in a large puddle of water with her legs wide opened, holding her stomach blowing as fast as she could in between her name-calling. Ty pleaded with her to try to calm down. He promised her everything was going to be okay.

"Yeah, that's the lie you told me the night your ass fucked me and got me pregnant," Terri growled.

Ty wasn't sure how he was going to get Terri to the hospital. He became confused and unsure of what to do. The only thing he was sure of was that he couldn't drive and as time passed with Terri yelling at the top of her lungs, he became overwhelmed. He walked to the other side of the room where Terri couldn't see him. Just as tears welled up in his eyes, he heard a siren screaming from a distance. Thank God! "Terri, it's going to be okay, baby, help is on the way," Ty said as he ran out of the bedroom toward the front door. He prayed he was right. As he yanked open the front door, he struggled through the snow to get into the middle of the street. Once there he saw a plow truck clearing the way for a fire truck that wasn't far behind. *Shit! It's a fuckin' fire truck. There's no fire on this street. What the fuck!* he thought. Anger smoldering, he turned to struggle back to his front door when a loud voice boomed through a bullhorn, "*Freeze!*"

It startled Ty and he fell face-first into the snow. As he was trying to get back on his feet two firemen approached and took position left to right of him to help him up. As they both helped him to his feet the firefighter to his right said, "Sir, are you, Mr. Spaulding?"

Breathing heavy and trying to catch his breath, Ty barked, "Yes!"

"My name is Captain Hernandez and to your left is Sergeant Dickerson. Mr. Spaulding, where is your wife?"

Ty said, "My wife, what!"

"Mr. Spaulding, we're here to take your wife to the hospital," Captain Hernandez said.

"Oh, oh my God! She's inside in the back bedroom. Please hurry!" Once inside Ty said, "Hey, hey wait, how are you guys going to take my wife to the hospital in a fire truck?"

"Mr. Spaulding, trust us, this isn't our first time. Now please, take us to your spouse."

Just as they entered the bedroom, JC said in an audible tone, "Ty, we're in Garysburg." Ty woke up groggy, dazed, and confused, wiping the drool from his chin and grinning from ear to ear. Several seconds later he was back on point, and his grin dropped.

Chapter 15

'I GOT THIS

JC turned off the screamer when they were thirty miles outside of Garysburg, North Carolina. He decided to ease into town. He didn't want to give anybody the wrong impression. They needed help and he was determined to get it. This situation was very personal.

When they arrived in Garysburg, they went straight to the Garysburg Police Department. John Cole walked into the Garysburg PD and flashed his badge and rattled off his credentials rapidly just like he was still an FBI agent. The desk sergeant seemed somewhat confused. He looked from JC to Ty and said, "What can I do for you, gentlemen?"

JC calmed himself by slowing his breathing and said, "Is the chief in?"

The desk sergeant paused for several seconds, and then asked the two gentlemen to have a seat as he slapped his right ear and rattled off a few words.

Captain Gregory busted through the set of double doors and barked, "Who are you two?" JC jumped to his feet extending his right hand to shake. Captain Gregory was somewhat reluctant to exchange the gesture. JC gave him the same intro as he did with the desk sergeant, just a little slower. Captain Gregory nodded and said, "Follow me."

"So, what can I do for you two gentlemen?" JC gave the intro on their way to Captain Gregory's office. Once inside his office Captain Gregory asked the two men to have a seat as he went around the desk to his high-back leather chair. JC told the captain why they were there. Fifteen minutes into the story, Captain Gregory leaned forward while raising his finger, he asked JC to hold on. Captain Gregory rattled off several codes into an intercom ending by saying, "In five, Sergeant Patterson!"

Chapter 16

'I GOT YOU

Terri was beside herself. Ty wasn't answering his cell phone. She had no idea what was going on. This upset her. *Why isn't he letting me know what's going on?* she wondered. She decided to have another vodka and orange juice. As time slowly ticked by, Terri became more agitated. She started pacing the floor like a confused psycho, saying over and over, "The do-gooder always gets fucked."

She decided to try that friend of Tycie's again. *Maybe she forgot to tell me something. Yeah, that's it, she forgot to tell me something,* she thought.

Terri found Gloria's number and dialed frantically. It seemed like the phone rang ten times before this unnecessarily excited voice politely said, "How are you, Mrs. Spaulding?" The return exchange from Terri was less enthusiastic.

"Gloria, have you heard from Tycie?"

"No, ma'am, not sense the other day as I told you before."

"Oh my God!" Gloria blurted as she grabbed her mouth.

"Mrs. Spaulding, you still haven't heard from Tycie?" she managed to get out.

"Hell no!" Terri yelled as she raised her trembling right hand to her lips, took a deep drag from her joint, and threw her head back, slowly exhaling, blowing the smoke into the air. There were several seconds of dead air and then, "We still haven't heard from her" Terri yelled.

Gloria didn't like her tone, but out of respect for her best friend, she took in several deep breaths. "Mrs. Spaulding, I've told you all I know about Tycie's last call to me. I'm just as concerned and worried as you are. She's my best friend. I wish I did know more, but I don't. Why would I hold back on any information that would help find her?" Gloria said as calmly as she could trying to hold back tears. Mrs. Spaulding didn't reply, her bottom lip trembled as she squeezed her cell phone. A couple of seconds later Gloria said, "Would you like me to come to Kentucky—?"

Terri cut her off, and snapped, "Give a bitch a break. You'll just be in the way," and clicked off. Gloria just stared at her cell phone with her mouth hanging open in disbelieve. She recalled Tycie saying her mother had issues, but she didn't realize how bad she was until now.

Terri threw her cell phone across the room in disgust. She needed to pull herself together. *Everything is going to be fine*, she thought. She decided to smoke another joint to calm her nerves. After a few hits, she started to feel more relaxed. She then decided to pour herself another Grey Goose and juice. She went back into the family room and dropped down on the love seat, took another hit of her joint, and as she was resting her head on the back of the loveseat, her cell phone rang. The touch screen brought Ty's name and picture full screen. Terri loved this picture of him. He was dressed in all black, which turned her on. By the fourth ring, she answered with her sexy voice.

Ty spoke in a very low monotone. Terri's drink dropped from her hand to the floor and shattered. She instantly became worried; Ty usually spoke calm and low when there was a serious problem. She had to strain to hear him. He calmly shared the information that Sergeant Patterson shared with him and JC. Terri started to sob, Ty asked her to please stay calm. "Let's just keep this simple. They weren't sure of anything yet." He told her he called because he felt it was the right thing to do. It had been hours since they last spoke. Terri made Ty promise to call once he has seen the body. He assured her he would and hung up. Terri couldn't move; she sat there with the cell phone glued to her ear in a trance.

The doorbell rang, Terri jumped and dropped the cell phone. She had to refocus; this isn't doing anybody any good. She gathered herself, picked up her phone, and walked to the front door while yelling, "Who is it?"

The voice on the other side of the door said, "It's me, Terri, Rae!" Terri worked on getting herself together as she walked toward the front door. She mumbled, "Shit, shit, shit" with every step she took. When Terri opened the door, she was in tears. Rae stepped through the front door with both arms extended mouthing, "Bug-a-boo, I'm here, I just heard."

The two embraced and held one another for a few seconds. They both seemed somewhat reluctant to let go of one another as they sniffed and tried to outcry each other. As they separated, they both said in unison, "What have you heard?"

They both took a step back and looked into one another eyes, smiled and embraced again as Terri said, "Please, come in, girl. I'm glad you're here."

Rae stepped into the house and said, "Have you heard from Ty or JC?"

Closing the door and turning, Terri said, "I just got off the phone with Ty. There's an unidentified body in that county's morgue. Ty felt it was only fair, that I knew before he and JC went to see if they could identify the body."

"Oh my God," Rae muttered.

"If that's my Tycie, I don't know what I'll do," Terri managed to say with a weak voice.

"Don't think like that. Calm down. It's going to be okay. I believe in JC and Ty. They'll chase this rabbit until they catch it," Rae whispered. The two walked into the kitchen area. Rae put her coat on the back of the barstool and said, "I could use a hit of that joint, and what you got to drink?"

Chapter 17

FOR THE THINKING IMPAIRED

Seth jumped behind the wheel of the Mercedes-Benz and froze. Several minutes later he decided to see what was in the fridge to eat. He had time, he thought. After all, he hadn't had anything to eat since yesterday and he was starving. He jumped out of the Mercedes-Benz and went back into the kitchen through the garage door. When he opened the refrigerator, his eyes lit up as he glared at six beers. He grabbed a bottle of Hoegaarden and attempted to read the label to himself, "Ho Gar Den." He liked the way that sounded. The correct pronunciation is (Who Gar Den). He popped the top and took a deep swig of "Who Gar Den," finishing it off with an *ahhh* and loud belch. As he popped open another one, he said, smiling from ear to ear, "This is my new Ho of choice!" He lit a joint, took a couple of puffs, and dropped into the lounge chair in the large comfortable space. He thought to himself, *this is the life, I could stay here forever.*

Five bottles and two joints later, he was fucked-up and still hungry. He finally built up enough energy to get out of the lounge chair. Once on his feet, he decided to check out the rest of the house. Stumbling from room to room, he had a smile from ear to ear. *This place is huge,* he thought. *Cracker Jack and what's her name did a good job of cleaning out the place.*

He stumbled back into the kitchen and fell into the refrigerator door. He quickly stepped back and snatched the door opened. He grabbed all the lunch meat, cheese, fruit, bread, and anything else that looked good to his over-the-top hunger. The food was thrown about on the table. Seth dropped into the chair at the head of the table and stuffed his face as fast as he could. He destroyed whatever was in sight. As he filled, his eyes got heavy, he rested his head on the back of the chair and closed his eyes.

After a few minutes his eyes popped open, he was wide-eyed, he sat straight up and said to himself, *Self, why have I been so stupid?* Self-came back with, *Stupid is what stupid does. There must be more to this*, he thought. Cracker Jack had gone way out on this one and he scored damn good. *Why had it seemed so easy*, he thought? Cracker Jack was very much in control of this situation, whatever it was. Seth ate and thought until he chewed himself into a deep sleep.

Chapter 18

LIFE TOOK OVER FOR A MINUTE

While waiting on Sergeant Patterson, Captain Gregory updated Ty and JC on the unknown body they had in the morgue. He broke down the crime scene as easily as he could. JC and Ty became very uneasy. As Captain Gregory continued, Ty said, "Oh my God," while grabbing his face, "this could be my girl."

Just as JC attempted to comfort Ty, Sergeant Patterson blew through the door barking, "Captain, I got here as quickly as I could." Captain Gregory thanked him, introduced him to JC and Ty, and concluded the intro with, "Let's go." The men jumped to their feet and followed Captain Gregory through the squad room out to the parking garage.

Sergeant Patterson opened the passenger door. When Captain Gregory was in, Sergeant Patterson closed his door and ran around the rear of the car to the driver side, got in, and put on the screamer as he burned out of the parking garage.

The men didn't speak as they drove to the morgue. Ty's mind was racing 100 miles per hour. He was so worried about how Terri would take the bad news. He felt bad that he wouldn't be there to hold her through the initial shock of trying to understand what may have happened. JC was very concerned about Ty's reaction once they saw the body. *He's been through enough, but can I handle this? I love her too,* JC thought.

Captain Gregory could not imagine how he would handle this situation if it were his son or daughter. The thought made him shiver. He prayed this young woman was not Mr. Spaulding's daughter, Tycie. When Sergeant Patterson pulled the screamer up to the front door of the morgue, Captain Gregory jumped out, Ty and JC followed suit.

As they walked into the small space to identify the body Ty asked for a few minutes. He closed his eyes and took a few moments to pray. As he opened his eyes, he grabbed his cell phone out of his pocket and speed-dialed Terri. In the middle of the second ring, Terri had the cell phone to her ear saying, "Ty, oh my God."

He softly said, "I'm in the room to identify the body, but I now realize that I can't do this without you. She's our girl. I need you on the phone with me when I identify our baby's body." She gasped, paused for a few seconds before saying, "I'm here." Ty looked at Captain Gregory and nodded. Captain Gregory pushed a button alongside the window and said, "Okay."

It seemed like it took hours for the curtain to rise completely; it was dark. Within a few seconds, a light came on. Ty gasped and before he could say anything, Terri blurted out, "Oh my God!"

JC turned quickly and grabbed Ty, mouthing "oh my God" with nothing coming out. Both men teared up as they embraced and did the double pat back-to-back together.

As they paused, Ty bounced back into the conversation with Terri. He softly said, "It's not Tycie…. Oh my God, Terri, it's not Tycie." He stiffened as he tried to calm himself. After thanking God over and over, he finally realizes he should calm himself down. There was a young nude mutilated and sodomized body lying before him. He snapped back into father mode and told Terri he'd call her right back.

Ty looked at Captain Gregory and said, "Captain this isn't my daughter, Tycie." He turned and walked out of the small space. As he walked toward the water fountain, he slowly exhaled, grabbed his cell phone, and speed-dialed Terri. She answered, he could tell she had been crying. Ty said, "Hey, Terri," in his best upbeat voice. Before she could respond, he jumped right into what had just taken place.

Terri took a deep breath and slowly exhaled, "Thank God!" As her eyes were becoming moist, she said, "Call me when you find our daughter" and clicked off without a goodbye. Ty stood there holding a dead phone to his ear with his mouth hanging open in midsentence.

JC walked up behind Ty, put his arm around his shoulder, and asked if Terri was okay. Ty just looked over at him with a blank look on his face. Just as JC was about to ask what's wrong, Captain Gregory walked up and said, "That's good news for you two but bad news for the department and whoever the parents are of that poor innocent mutilated body of Jane Doe. We're back at square one. Don't get me wrong, I'm glad it isn't your daughter. That poor girl has been taken away from this world by some sick-minded wacko that doesn't have a soul. We will catch the sick bastard. That young woman has my word on that."

Back at the station, Captain Gregory asked JC and Ty, "Where do you go from here?" While JC gave that question some thought, Ty sat there with his face in his hands. JC jumped to his feet thanking Captain Gregory and Sergeant Patterson for their time. Ty stood and extended his hand as he, too, thanked Captain Gregory and Sergeant Patterson. They both wished the two men the best of luck and Captain Gregory went on to say, "If there is anything else that I and my department can do, feel free to give me a call." Both men thanked him and left.

JC had Buster wide open with the siren screaming, headed back to Kentucky. Ty asked, "What now?"

"Home," JC said.

"Home to do what?" Ty snapped.

JC said in a low tone, "Don't worry, man. It's going to be okay, I promise."

Chapter 19

WHY INVITE ME TO YOUR NIGHTMARE

Just as JC approached exit 91A-B Western KY Parkway Elizabethtown Paducah, Ty said, "Take me to Tycie's place." JC didn't say a word; he did as Ty asked. As they drove along Ty didn't say another word. Turning into Tycie's subdivision brought Ty back to life. He sat up and looked around the neighborhood like he had never been there before.

JC pulled into Tycie's driveway and before he could cut off the car Ty jumped out and headed to the front door, grabbing the keys from his jacket pocket. Just as he put the key into the lock, JC was by his side. As JC closed the front door, Ty stopped in his tracks. Something didn't seem right, just as the thought crossed his mind, he whispered, "Oh my God!"

JC whipped his Glock from his side, gripped Ty's shoulder, and slowly moved him aside. He slowly moved down the hall scaling along the wall with his Glock cocked and ready to take a motherfucker-out! Just as JC stepped around the corner into the kitchen, Seth uncontrollably stood straight up from the table drawing a weapon as JC shouted freeze and pulled the trigger before Seth could utter a word, his lifeless body dropped back into the chair.

JC signaled to Ty to stay put. He did a sweep of the first floor and slowly made his way up the back stairs from the kitchen. When he stepped into the last bedroom he dropped to the foot of the bed after he swept the room. This is not looking good at all. This situation was moving in the wrong direction. He loved Ty like a brother, but he had to tell him the truth. They have a serious problem.

Several minutes later Ty yelled out for JC in a low whisper. JC slowly got to his feet and yelled back, "All clear."

Ty ran up the stairs two at a time yelling, "Tycie's nowhere to be found?" JC met him in the hallway, Ty started going from room to room in a frantic while saying over and over, "God, no!"

JC sat on the top step and rested his face in both hands. Ty ran down the stairs yelling at the top of his lungs, "It looks like the place has been ransacked. Why, what in the fuck is going on? Where is Tycie?" *This can't be happening,* JC thought.

JC followed Ty down the stairs, yelling, "Don't touch anything. This is now a crime scene." JC grabbed his cell from his front pocket and hit "Emergency Call." In less than two minutes, JC rattled off, who he was, where they were, and what had taken place. When JC clicked off, he suggested the two of them go outside and wait in the car until the cops arrived.

Detective Lacey was the first to arrive on the scene...

Chapter 20

THE DO-GOODER GETS FUCKED

JC got out of the car introducing himself as Detective Lacey approached. Detective Lacey exchanged the intro and got down to business. "What happened here?" she barked. JC started his explanation from the point of entry into the home. Ty approached, introduced himself to Detective Lacey, and then rudely took over the conversation, rambling on. JC just closed his eyes and dropped his head. After a few seconds, he interrupted, "Detective Lacey, please forgive my friend, I think he's in shock."

"In shock about what? Nobody's telling me a goddamn thing."

JC cut off Detective Lacey by raising his voice and yelling out the explanation starting from where he left off before being interrupted by Ty as several other squad cars pulled up out screaming each other.

Detective Lacey yelled as loud as she could. "Kill the noise and lock down the crime scene. Nobody goes inside the house until I give the word. Detective Parker, you come with me, Detective Lacey ordered." As the four of them walked through the front door, Ty did all he could to hold himself together. This situation was way out of control. There were so many unanswered questions. He prayed to keep it together. He didn't want to come across as an uncontrolled wuss.

As they entered the house, JC jumped right into replay mode. He walked both detectives through what had played out once he and Ty entered the house. "Within seconds of being in the home, I realized something was wrong, I signaled to Ty to stay put," JC said. "As I stepped around the corner into the kitchen, this punk jumped to his feet as I yelled freeze, drawing a weapon."

"Did the victim say anything before you shot him?" Detective Lacey asked.

"No, as I came around the corner of the kitchen, this punk jumped to his feet drawing a weapon!" JC said. "Then once I took him out, I swiftly scanned the rest of the house. You know, Detective Lacey, like doing your job!" JC snapped. There was something about Detective Lacey's attitude that he didn't like. He just wasn't sure what it was.

Ty played back his first and last moments of entering the house and going back to the car. "Everything was flashing in front of me as we move from the second floor to the first. So many of Tycie's things were gone from room to room. I was confused and unsure of what was going on. The next thing I knew, JC was on the phone talking fast and telling me we need to go wait in the car until the brass arrives. This is my daughter's house!" he yelled. "She's missing, and this punk is sitting at her table, with food and beer bottles all over the place and my daughter is nowhere to be found. What's going on? Where is my daughter!"

"Sir, how long has your daughter been missing?" Detective Lacey questioned. "What's going on here, retired FBI agent John Craig Cole? Because one plus zero is not two, stated more like a statement than a question. Talk to me, man! My department never got a missing person report for this residence."

Detective Lacey took a couple of steps toward JC, stopped, and said, with clenched teeth, "This whole thing sucks! Let me play this bullshit back. Okay, let me get this straight. "You two strolled your asses to the front door, and you Ty inserted the key into the lock, walked in and this strange guy jumps up from the table with a gun, and you, JC, shoot him? Before either could respond, she went on. You're trying to tell me that this is how this shit played out?" Before JC or Ty could answer, Detective Lacey stepped off yelling orders over her shoulder, "Maybe you two should think about getting yourselves a lawyer. Detective Parker, get the forensic team in here. Sergeant Sanchez, read Mr. Cole and Mr. Spaulding their Miranda rights and take the two of them back to the precinct and get their statements in separate interview rooms starting from day one to the present.

Oh…don't forget to file a missing person report if that's confirmed by the evidence!"

Chapter 21

CRANK IT DOWN

Rae and Terri both clicked off their cell phone. Terri just sat there looking into space. "Thank God," Rae said.

"Thank God?" Terri replied. "Tycie is still missing, why are we thanking God?"

"Why not?" Rae said. "That poor girl in that morgue isn't Tycie. There's still hope that everything is okay."

"Hope? She is still missing. Tycie doesn't just disappear. If she doesn't communicate anything to me, she communicates with her father. This isn't like her!" Terri yammered.

Rae jumped to her feet. "Okay, let's both calm down. I'll fix us another drink. Take a hit of that joint to settle your nerves. I'm not the enemy. This is just a small setback; JC will not let this slow him down. He's not going to stop searching until he finds her, you can take that fact to the bank, my sista."

"I hear you," Terri managed to say while trying to hold in the smoke from the joint she just hit. While choking and coughing she mouthed, "The problem is when, where, and how, as a couple of large puffs of smoke escaped from between her lips."

Just as Rae returned with the drinks, the doorbell rang. Terri's eyes bugged as she jumped out of fear from the sound of the doorbell. "Who in the fuck can that be?" she blurted out. As Terri got up to answer the door, she told Rae to get rid of the weed and spray.

As Terri stumbled toward the door yelling "who is it," she noticed her reflection in the mirror as she was passing it and stopped in her tracks for several seconds, just staring at herself. She had aged overnight. She looked old and beat down; she barely recognized herself. This situation was weighing her down. Terri sucked her teeth, shook her head, and stepped off. As she approached the front door, she heard the person on the other side of the door calling out to her.

"Mrs. Spaulding! It's me."

As she snatched open the door, she shouted, "Me who!" She couldn't believe it. Her lips tightened as she said, "What in the hell are you doing here?"

Gloria stepped through the door and embraced Terri while asking, "Have you heard anything?"

Terri angrily pushed away, took a couple of steps back to put space between her and Gloria, and retorted, "What in the hell are you doing here?"

Gloria grimly said, "Under the circumstances, I couldn't stay away. I didn't know Tycie was still missing until I spoke with you earlier today."

"So? That doesn't explain to me why you felt a sudden urge to fly your ass all this way," Terri argued.

"Please, Mrs. Spaulding, let's not do this now. My concerns are all about Tycie. Can we put our differences aside?" Gloria said.

Before Terri could reply, Rae walked up asking, "Who is it?" When Gloria saw Rae, her eyes lit up. She walked over toward Rae with her arms stretched out. The two embraced. "Oh my God, Gloria, how are you?" Rae asked as the two separated.

"Just fine," Gloria replied with a smile from ear to ear. Gloria suddenly turned to remember her spouse was still standing in the doorway. As she gestured her way, she made an apology and said, "This is Karen Kirkwood, my partner."

Terri muttered, "Your partner. Is that a new term to justify your sin?"

The two young women looked at one another as Rae said, "Come on in, I'm sure you're both drained after that flight." They both thanked her and followed her toward the family room. As Terri was closing the door, she said with attitude, "Yeah, come on in" and slammed the door.

Rae had always been fond of Gloria. She was glad to see her, however, she was surprised to learn about the partner. The last conversation between her and Tycie led her to believe that Gloria was alone and lonely and had been for a few years. Rae took their coats and overnight bag.

"Have a seat, would you two like something to drink?" Rae offered. Karen, nicknamed KK said, "Do you have any Chives Regal?"

Rae said, "Yes we do."

KK said, "Can I have that neat?"

Rae walked toward the bar while saying, "And, Gloria, would you like Kahlua on the rocks?"

Gloria hesitated for a second before saying, "No thanks. I'll have a shot of Cognac."

Rae paused for a bit before saying, "I'm sorry, that question was for Terri."

Terri looked at Rae and angrily smoldered, "You know damn well my drink is vodka and juice."

Rae chuckled and said doggedly, "Just testing, my Sista." When Rae stepped behind the bar, she felt somewhat uncomfortable. She took a few minutes to get herself together before fixing the drinks. Rae brought the drinks over on a tray and sat them down on the coffee table. The women picked up their drinks as they thanked Rae. Rae decided on a toast. Here's to Tycie's safe return.

In unison, Gloria and KK said, "To Tycie's safe return."
Terri didn't utter a word. She just sat there looking into space.
Rae interrupted her thoughts by clearing her throat. Terri's
head snapped towards Rae.

"What, is something wrong?" Terri asked Rae.

"No, I had something in my throat."

Terri said, "Yeah, right." Terri went on. "So, you two just
decided to jump on a plane, and here you are."

Gloria put a hand on KK's leg and said, "Yup, here we
are!" As Gloria went on, Rae found herself thinking back to
her Georgia State days.

It seemed like only yesterday she thought...

Chapter 22

HOLD THAT THOUGHT

Rae had been a cop on the beat for several years when she decided being a cop on the beat wasn't enough. Her decision to attend law school was one of her best decisions to date. Having obtained a bachelor's degree in criminal justice before becoming a police officer meant only three years at Georgia State University College of Law (GSU), not more than four. That day the decision was made.

It was her third year (3L) and all her time was spend studying. Her favorite spot to study was Barnes & Noble. Over the last couple of years, Rae couldn't find her way home without stopping there to study for a few hours and complete an assignment. The atmosphere was pleasant, and Starbucks was within eyeshot.

A couple of months into her 3L at Georgia State, Rae noticed another young woman that would spend just as much time at Barnes & Noble as she did. They both seemed to sit in the same spot each time they stopped in to study. Wow, she was really in the zone, nothing seemed to distract her. Rae assumed she was probably a law student as well. *Maybe she's in her first year (1L), she does look rather young, but attractive,* she thought.

Rae decided to spend only a couple of hours tonight at Barnes & Noble working on her thesis. It was Friday and she had made up her mind during Professor Eisenhower's lecture that she would only do a couple of hours tonight and maybe go back on Saturday afternoon to finish whatever she didn't get done this evening. Professor Eisenhower's lecture usually put her in this frame of mind. If she could get through this, her last hurdle would be the bar exam and then on to officially practicing law. This made her feel excited. *It's been a long two and a half years*, she thought with a smile from ear to ear.

Just as she realized she was daydreaming she was looking into the eyes of the young attractive woman that sat at the other usual spot. The young woman exchanged the smile as she got up from her spot and walked toward Rae's. Before Rae could get her thoughts together the young woman was at her table extending her hand while rattling off her full name Gloria Kowalski. Rae jumped to her feet so fast she almost turned the small table over. Still smiling, she extended her hand and shared the exchange. "Rae Wyatt." Both women, still smiling, stood silent for a few seconds before Gloria said, "I see you here almost every evening. You must be studying law." Rae looked somewhat puzzled as Gloria continued. "Being here almost every night tells me we, I said *we*, don't have time for a social life."

Rae laughed shyly while nodding her head, and replying, "Oh yeah, right, right. You too! Huh."

"Yep," Gloria said. "My first year. How 'bout you?"

"My last, I hope. I'm working on my last assignment before the final hurdle," and before she could finish her sentence, they both said in unison, "The bar exam!" They both got a kick out of that.

Two hours later both women were still standing in the same spot exchanging stories about their experience at GSU. Rae was using her hands to illustrate her point when she noticed the time. She stopped in midsentence and gasped, grabbing her mouth and blurting out, "Look at the time. Oh my goodness."

Gloria chimed in with, "You've got to be kidding. Where did those two hours go?" she boomed with a broad smile, her left hand flying in the air and her right-hand resting cozy over her flat abdomen.

"I'm so sorry," Rae quickly said. "I've kept you from your work."

"No, no I've enjoyed our conversation," Gloria quickly said. "Like I told you a couple of hours ago, my plan for this evening is to treat myself to a mouthwatering dinner and a play. It's been a long hard week. It's Friday night and I need to wind down," Rae said with a beautiful smile that seemed to light up space around them both.

"Hey, why don't I join you, if you don't mind?" Gloria said.

"Sure," Rae boomed. "I would love to have you join me. Wait, wait, what about your assignment that's due on Monday?"

"Well," Gloria said, "I have all day tomorrow and Sunday. Besides, what I've learned from you in the last couple of hours has helped me put this year into perspective. So, that being said, let's go to dinner. I see this as a wise decision."

Chapter 23

YOU ARE SO SPECIAL

Both women sat down at the small table to hash over the plans for the evening. "I made reservations at Bibs Restaurant, nonetheless, it doesn't mean I'm not flexible, any ideas?"

Gloria said, "Great! Is this the one on Piedmont Avenue?"

"Yes, that's one of my favorite places. I enjoy the mixed grill and they have a wine selection to die for."

"Girl, I know what you mean. I'm with you on the wine, but when it's time to yum-yum the tum-tum, I'm all over the seared scallops, my sista."

"I hear you, gurl!" They smiled at one another and did the right-hand fist bump.

Gloria arrived at Bib's fifteen minutes early and backed into a corner parking spot. She decided to stay in the car until 7:00 p.m. to get herself together. She was excited about the rest of the evening. She still couldn't believe how long the two of them stood there talking. *Where had the time gone?* she marveled. It didn't matter. *We were both into the conversation and that's what counts,* she thought.

I wonder why she was staring at me when I looked up to go to the bathroom. What was on her mind? Shit, I'm glad I decided to go to the bathroom! The thought made her smile. *I admired the way she kept eye contact as she used her hands to illustrate her point. That talent comes from confidence. She's going to make a good attorney. She's smart, polite, and attractive. Damn, say it ain't so! Wow, I can work with that,* she confirmed to herself, shaking her head up and down, with a broad smile.

Just as Gloria finished her thought, she noticed Rae walking across the parking lot. Gloria jumped out of the car calling out to Rae. Rae stopped, turned, and smiled when she saw it was Gloria. "Hey, did you just get here?"

"A few minutes ago," Gloria replied.

The two women walked into Bib's together.

Rae was greeted at the door by the host, Mr. Edward. His smile introduced a gap wide enough for you to see halfway down his throat. After a good evening, he said, "Your usual table, Ms. Wyatt?"

"Of course, Mr. Edward, and how are you this evening?"

"Me and the family are doing just fine. My oldest starts college this fall."

"Congratulations," Rae said in an over joyful tone.

As Mr. Edward seated the two women, he thanked Rae and announced, "Your waiter will be with you momentarily." Rae thanked him and told him she would see him soon. She had kept that promise at least once a month. The only difference this time? She wasn't alone.

When Joshua came over to the table, he said, "Good evening, Ms. Wyatt. Would you like to start the evening off with a glass of your favorite white wine?"

"Yes, please."

Joshua looked in Gloria's direction and said, "And you, ma'am?"

Gloria said, "I'll have the same."

It seems like they were just sharing how good the meal was when Joshua approached the table saying, "Excuse me. Ms. Wyatt, I'm sorry to interrupt your conversation, but we're closed."

Both women looked at Joshua as though he were a stranger before saying, "Oh, we're so sorry."

Rae said, "Please bring me the check."

Gloria said, "No, I got mine." Rae insisted.

As they were walking through the parking lot, Gloria said, "I feel bad for making you miss the play."

"Girl, please, you didn't put a gun to my head to make me stay. I enjoyed your company."

"I as well yours," Gloria said in an audible tone. I tell you what, if you're not ready to call it a night, neither am I. It's still Friday night. How 'bout a movie at my place?"

Rae said, "No, I couldn't impose."

Gloria said, "Oh come on, I just downloaded *Blue Hill Avenue*. Trust, it's getting a lot of great reviews."

Rae said, "I meant to catch that at the theater."

Gloria said, "Well, now you can catch it at my house for free." They both laughed. Gloria rattled off her address and said, "Just follow me."

"I'm behind you," Rae said, beaming.

Chapter 24

HITTING THE SWEETEST NOTES

Gloria had a beautiful loft in Buckhead Georgia. When they walked into the loft, Gloria hit a switch that put on a couple of lights and started playing jazz from the speakers around the huge space. "Come on in; make yourself at home."

"Thanks, this is lovely. How long have you lived here?" Rae asked.

"Georgia is my home. I've lived in this apartment for several years," Gloria said.

"It's beautiful, may I?"

"Yes, please, make yourself at home."

Rae walked into the wide space admiring the surroundings with a smile from ear to ear as she rested her purse and shawl in the corner of the love seat. As she inspected the huge space like an inspector, her posture screamed impressed. Gloria's space was tastefully decorated. The Asian art that hung freely throughout the space was gorgeous. All that being emphasized by high-gloss hardwood floors and brick walls from top to bottom. Between two dark oakwood pillars was a cherrywood table with six straight-back chairs, centered on a two-step marble platform.

To the left was a 70-inch flatscreen mounted to the wall with a ten-speed bike hanging to the right above two floodlights, next to the fireplace with a closed-in glass smoked bathroom catty-cornered. The space across the room introduced a California/German king-size cherrywood ski bed with matching end tables and an antique trunk at the foot of the bed. On the wall to the left of that were racks of clothes. Some clothes were thrown about the bedroom space, but Gloria didn't make any apologies.

"Wine?" Gloria asked. Rae was a little hesitant. "I think I've had enough; I have to drive home."

"No you don't!" Gloria said before she could catch herself.

Rae just stared at her for a few seconds before clumsily saying, "What was it that you have to...drink?"

The two of them sat together in front of the fireplace without a word. After a few seconds, they both started to speak at the same time, which made them laugh. When they stopped laughing, they were facing each other. Gloria gently touched Rae's left cheek as she guided her face towards hers. They both stopped within inches of one another, smiled, and their lips gently came together.

Chapter 25

I'M COMING

As they enjoyed one another's soft lips and warm tongues, it was as though they were both slowly processing what was going on. Gloria pulled away slightly and looked Rae into her watering eyes and mouthed, "are you sure?" Rae responded to Gloria by pulling her back into her mouth.

Gloria whispered in Rae's ear how much she wanted to make love to her. Rae closed her eyes while praying, "God, please let this beautiful woman take advantage of me."

Gloria kissed Rae along her long, sweet neck, begging please, pausing for several seconds as she got closer and closer to her cleavage. Her body scent made Gloria wet, her moaning made her clitoris hard. Gloria gently laid Rae down on the floor and got on top of her. As they enjoyed one another, they started removing their clothes.

Seconds before their warm nude bodies came together, Gloria separated the lips of her vagina to expose her thriving hard clitoris. Rae followed suit as she slightly raised her hips and the tip of their wet clitoris and warm bodies connected. They melted in each other's arms as they moved together in a slow-motion rhythm. They were both so wet and hard. Their breathing increased as their bodies started to tremble. Rae begged Gloria not to stop. Gloria pulled Rae in closer as they shared the joy of the orgasm. They couldn't stop giving themselves to one another, they shared orgasm after orgasm!

Just as Rae was about to have another orgasm her mood was interrupted by a loud *ding dong!* As she abruptly refocused, she realized she was at her dear friend's in support of her missing daughter, her goddaughter. She automatically blurted out, "I'll get it!" As Rae, briskly stepped away from the gathering, legs tight, to keep the moistness from running down her legs, she approached the door, blurting, "Who is it!"

Chapter 26

NOBODY CARES WHAT YOU THINK

Rae snatched the door opened, yelling can I help you. Detective Lacey flashed her department ID while clipping off her credentials rapidly. Rae stepped back yelling, "Oh my God. Something has happened to Tycie!"

Terri jumped to her feet, pushing Gloria and KK out of her way, and clumsily stumbled to the front door yelling, "*Please say it's not so!*"

Detective Lacey stepped through the door while asking the ladies to please calm down. "I have no evidence of Tycie's disappearance. I'm here about Mr. John Cole and Tyrone Spaulding hanging out in Elizabethtown at 9890 Sunningdale Road with a corpse sitting humped over at a kitchen table with his face in a table of some shit he may have had the night before. A dead man and two crying grown men, one claiming his daughter's disappeared. I'm having a problem putting the two together. A dead man and two grown crying men."

Terri stepped into Detective Lacey's space and said with her teeth clenched, "That crying man, Tyrone Spaulding, happens to be my husband looking for our missing daughter, Tycie."

"So, they're telling the truth," Detective Lacey said.

"Hell yeah! They're telling the damn truth!" Rae said, just as upset as Terri. "Now tell us, Ms. Detective, what in the fuck are you here for, corpse, Ty, JC, what!"

"Okay like I said, calm the fuck down. So, Mrs. Spaulding, your daughter is missing?"

Terri yelled at the top of her lungs, "YES!"

"Please, Mrs. Spaulding, can we have a seat?"

"Yes, just tell me what this is all about, if it isn't my daughter why were you at my daughter's home! Where is my damn husband?"

"I had them both taken to the precinct for questioning."

"Questioning?" Rae and Terri said in unison.

"I need the two of you to come down to the precinct."

"Precinct!" Terri said.

"Yes," Detective Lacey went on. "There are a lot of unanswered questions. Just to name a few, why hasn't a missing person been filed for your daughter, why is a corpse in her house, why is a friend of a family member now being charged with murder and forever tagged as a killer? Under the circumstances, I think that's more than enough for me to haul all your Black asses in. I'm trying hard to be nice about this shit. Now, if I must take other actions, I'll have to call for backup."

Terri stood abruptly and said, "Detective Lacey, you're not going to come into my house and throw your bullshit around. Gloria, you and KK go ahead upstairs and make yourselves at home. You know where the guestroom is. Rae, you and I will follow Detective Lacey in my car." As Detective Lacey started to speak, Terri cut her off by saying in a sarcastic tone, "Do we need fucking attorneys?"

Detective Lacey shot back, while standing, "Your husband and his friend may" and stormed out of the house.

Chapter 27

YOU JUST DON'T GET IT, IT FALLS ON DEAF EARS

Ty and JC were sitting in separate small spaces facing a large mirror, with no windows, and one other chair. Ty had his right elbow on the table nibbling on his fingertips and his left leg moving up and down a mile a minute. *It seems like I've been in this small space for hours. I need to get out of here and find my daughter!* Ty thought. He couldn't believe the mayhem he and JC walked into when they entered the house. It had been ransacked; a strange-looking man was sitting at the table as if he lived there. *What in the fuck is going on? Where is my daughter?* He banged both fists on the table as he abruptly stood, the chair flew back, banging up against the wall, and he dropped his face into his cupped hands just as the door swung opened.

Detective Lacey stepped into the boxed-in space on the other side of the mirror. "What we got Sanchez?" she barked.

"Nothing yet. Chief said to save them for you."

She hit the sergeant on his shoulder while saying, "Thanks, I'm going in."

Detective Lacey stepped through the narrow doorway saying to Ty, "Remember me?"

Ty's head popped up and he replied, "You think? How could I fucking forget you. I need to get out of here so that I can find my daughter."

"Yes, Mr. Spaulding, your daughter, let's talk about your daughter. I understand you've been given your Miranda rights."

"Yes," Ty said.

"Good, okay, Mr. Spaulding, how did we get here?" Detective Lacey asked.

Ty cleared his throat and started from the initial call from Terri. As he was going through the story as he recalled, he seemed somewhat hesitant, he was trying to keep his head in the game as he stumbled through what took place after he and JC entered the house. "When JC yelled all clear from upstairs, I took the steps two at a time to get to Tycie's bedroom, shit was all over the place, it didn't look like Tycie's room. JC was sitting on the edge of Tycie's bed, with a 'deer in the headlight' look. 'She's not here, I checked all the rooms, no Tycie,' JC said. All I could say was 'You sure?' 'I'm sure,' he replied. 'Don't touch anything, we need to call the cops.' JC grabbed his cell phone from his back pocket as he stood up from the bed, headed out of the room, down the stairs, and out the front door. I was on the back of his heels. You know the rest," Ty said.

Detective Lacey looked at Ty for several seconds, stood said, "Yeah, right, I know the rest," turned, and walked out of the small space as Ty was yelling, "Detective wait!"

Detective Lacey was on the other side of the mirror standing next to Sergeant Sanchez, with both hands in her pockets. After a few seconds, she turned and said, "Let them both go and tell them not to leave town, not even to look for his daughter. The wife came down and filed a missing person report. We'll be taking on the case. After their release, come to my office, we have a lot of lost time to makeup. It's been over seventy-two hours, were behind the time frame, we need to hustle."

Sargent Sanchez escorted Ty and JC to the waiting area. Both women jumped to their feet and ran into their arms as they approached. "Oh my God, Ty, what's going on?" Terri asked.

Ty looked into Terri's bloodshot eyes and said in a whisper, "Not here, let's go to your place." They convoyed home in silence.

Chapter 28

HERE COMES OLE STRANGER DANGER

The frail-framed woman stood on the catwalk shaking uncontrollably. Her bony knobby knees were knocking together, and her teeth were chattering. The large space was eerie, cold, musky, and dark. The oversized windows that were not broken out had black crud all over them. Shit dangled from the ceiling. Huge pipes, wooden barrels, and rubber hoses were scattered throughout the large space. Rats, mice, and critters scurried and bustled about blending into all the other weird noises that seemed to be booming in surround sound. The many puddles of water scattered throughout the space kept everything in harmony, *plop, plop, plop.* This whole scene screamed eerie. *How long are we going to be here?* Stump wondered.

Cracker Jack paced the large space like he was going to lose his mind any second. His head was down, his nasty blond hair hung down left to right covering his rugged face. He was sucking on cigarettes one after the other. A cloud of smoke hovered over his head as he walked the space. She didn't like him when he was like this. On edge, everybody was an enemy and every word seemed to have a different meaning than everybody else's. The cocaine surely wasn't helping the situation. The van was on the east side of the warehouse, still loaded. *Cracker Jack ain't telling me shit, the psycho motherfucker, what the fuck!* Stump thought.

Cracker Jack hadn't heard from Seth in over twenty-four hours, that wasn't like him when it came to money. *I know the greedy bastard was clear on our communications,* Cracker Jack thought. *Fuck him for now.* Cracker Jack snatched his cell phone out of his front pant pocket and jammed in several numbers. The voice on the other end answered in a very low raspy voice, "This is not a good time" and hung up. Cracker Jack yanked the phone from his ear and looked at the face of the phone, spit on it, and mumbled, "Bitch, nobody hangs up on me," squeezing the phone so tight the face cracked. Just as Stump started to yell down to Cracker Jack, he disappeared into the shadows.

It was bone-aching cold on this hard, foul, slimy-ass surface. She could only see darkness no matter how many times she bat her eyes. The right side of her face was numb laying in the slimy funky shit. She wasn't sure if her right eye was opened or closed; her hands and feet were tied together behind her back. Except for the trembling, her body was unfamiliar to her as she struggled to stay conscious. She felt like her head was going to explode, rats were running across her body and nibbling on her fingertips, at this point she couldn't feel a thing. She was still confused; she couldn't wrap her head around what was going on. Everything was running together.

Just as she was losing consciousness, something stepped into her space and startled her by grabbing her and throwing her against a wall like a rag doll, the impact knocked her unconscious and she started convulsing. Cracker Jack hustled across the slime and straddled the rag doll. He stuffed a nasty rag in her mouth to keep her from swallowing her tongue. He flipped her over and cut her hands and feet loose and rolled her onto her back. He pounced on her lifeless body. This time as he straddled her, he was unfastening his belt buckle, pants, and unzipping his zipper as he pulled out his nasty dripping dick.

He stroked his penis as he rubbed the tip of his dick against her stomach while pulling on her bloody nipple. just as he started shaking uncontrollably, he jammed his rock-solid dick into her dry lifeless pussy as he grabbed her around the neck and squeezed. As his heart started beating faster and faster, his thrusts got harder and harder as he finely ejaculated while yelling at the top of his lungs, "Fuck this bitch!" After a few seconds he stiffened, dropped down on her cold body, and went limp, gasping for air. He slowly got up off her badly beaten body, pulling his pants up. He kicked her as hard as he could in the ribs and spit on her and said, "You bitch! You can thank your mother for this shit!"

Cracker Jack gathered himself as he hustled over to the van, jumped in, and sped off.

Stump hobbled from the shadows and stood there for a few seconds until the van was out of sight.

Chapter 29

DRIVEN BY SOMETHING ELSE

They were all sitting there in silence with a drink when Gloria and KK walked in and Gloria said, "Oh my God, is Tycie okay?"

Ty looked up and said, "No, don't know, we're at a loss." As the two women walked in, they both got a drink and joined the others.

Terri's cell phone vibrated, and she excused herself and went into the kitchen to take the call. Ty asked, "Is everything okay?"

Terri replied, "Yes, if there's a problem, I'll let you know." When in the kitchen Terri said, "This is not a good time" and hung up.

Terri paced the length of the kitchen, trying to figure out what to do. Ty walked into the kitchen, ran up to Terri, and said, "What is it?"

"Our baby girl is missing, and we have no idea where she is!" Ty embraced Terri and assured her they would find Tycie.

Ty suggested they fix their guests something to eat. Terri, wiped her eyes and said, "Our guests?"

"Yes, our guests." The two walked out into the family space and said, "Please make yourselves comfortable. Dinner in one hour."

JC jumped to his feet and said, "It's been over twenty-four hours since my last meal."

Rae also jumped to her feet to support the idea of a good meal. "How about a nice wine with dinner?"

Terri said, "I'm out of wine."

Rae said, "No problem; I'll make a run to the liquor store."

"Great," Terri replied.

Rae turned and said, "Gloria, would you like to ride?"

This caught Gloria off guard. She turned toward KK and said, "Would you like something special?"

KK said, "Sure, grab me a bottle of wine." Gloria shared a warm smile with KK, kissed her, and said, "I know what you want."

KK looked Gloria in her eyes and said, "I know you do."

They smiled at one another, and Gloria said, "Hold that thought and I'll see you in a few."

While in the car, they were both silent. After several miles, Rae said, "So, how have you been?"

Gloria replied, "I don't think that's your business, as we agreed the last time we saw one another."

"You seem happy," Rae said.

Gloria, shot back, "I am, because I'm with a gay woman who loves me. Not a confused bisexual."

Rae said, "Okay, I deserve that. However, I do still love you."

"I don't need your one-sided love anymore."

"Please, I'm here for Tycie. I did not expect to see you. Let's leave it at that."

"I've moved on," Gloria said. "Just be happy for me."

Rae listened to what Gloria was saying and replied, "You're right. We agreed to move on without one another several years ago. I'm sorry, I hadn't seen or heard anything from you in so long; guess seeing you made me realize—"

Gloria cut Rae off by saying, "Let's focus on Tycie. I'm a happy gay woman and I'm not into bisexuals, period."

Chapter 30

WHO SAID SHE'S THE VOICE OF REASON?

Detective Lacey and Sergeant Sanchez, sat in her office going over the evidence they had on the Tycie Spaulding case. "What they had and what was said didn't make sense. What they are saying doesn't seem to match the evidence. Daddy 'Ty' changing the story from Mr. FBI being on the end of the bed, to the top of the stairs; There is something more going on with these people. I just can't put my finger on it." Sergeant Sanchez just listened to Detective Lacey as she laid out the evidence.

"Did you notice the reaction of the wife?" Detective Lacey asked.

Sergeant Sanchez said, "She seemed confused and unsure of what was going on."

"Exactly. She reacted robotically. It wasn't natural to me," Detective Lacey said. "I didn't see a tear for at least two minutes."

Sergeant Sanchez said, "Boss, we can't react based on what didn't happen. We must have more to go on."

Detective Lacey replied, "I know. Okay, what else do we have?"

"The two men make a trip to North Carolina, and they come back empty-handed. However, they did identify a body."

Detective Lacey said, "And what was the condition of the body?"

Sergeant Sanchez said, "They didn't get into the corpse other than, it wasn't Tycie." "Okay," Detective Lacey said, how much did you get out of the wife before the husband and his friend were released?"

"Nothing," Sergeant Sanchez replied.

"Let's stay on top of this; something just doesn't seem right," Detective Lacey said.

Sanchez agreed. "What's next?" he asked.

Detective Lacey thought about that before saying, "Get the team together. Meet me at the crime scene."

When they arrived back at the scene, Detective Lacey suggested each detective take a room and make sure no stone goes unturned.

The detectives replied, "Understood," and they went to work.

Chapter 31

TIMEOUT

It was getting late, they had eaten, drank, and shared old stories. Gloria and KK decided to call it a night. Terri suggested they make themselves at home and if they needed anything let her know.

JC, Rae, Terri, and Ty sat down at the dining room table and recapped the last forty-eight hours. None of this made sense to any of them. Tycie never just went off and left her family and friends in the dark. Ty was very reassuring. He suggested they all get some sleep and pick this up tomorrow.

JC turned to Rae and asked, "Are you going to stay here with Terri?"

Rae replied, "No, I'll see you at home."

JC said, "Okay," while standing and said, "Ty, I'll give you a ride home when you're ready."

Rae and Terri sat in silence until Rae said, "Gurl, I'm going to go. I'll be back first thing in the morning. If you need anything before then, just call and I'll be here in a flash." Terri walked Rae to the door, thanked her again with a hug. Rae assured her everything would be okay.

Terri walked into the kitchen and sat at the kitchen table. She thought about her last call. Something had gone wrong. She wasn't sure what, but she just had a bad feeling. This situation had gotten out of hand. Terri didn't expect all of this. *Gloria and her whatever she calls her, are here in my house, cops, corpses, and running up and down the highway.* Terri had to get a handle on this. *Things are way out of control.*

Chapter 32

HUMAN TRAMPOLINE

The boney-framed woman barely casting a shadow hobbled nervously toward the badly beaten body. As she approached, she noticed there was no movement from the poor girl. Stump just stood there looking down at what appeared to be a lifeless body. She kicked the woman several times telling her to wake up and got nothing.

Stump dropped her boney frame next to the cold body. She didn't understand why Cracker Jack was so off the charts on this one. He was acting as if this was personal, and she didn't understand that. But what she did understand, was that she had never agreed to murder. This was just another job, "like all the others," he'd said; he never said anything about murder or a third person.

Stump had to make some decisions; this shit was not looking good. Her eyes bugged as she recalled her backpack being left behind.

Cracker Jack took another swig out of the bottle as he thought about Seth. He could always depend on Seth. How did he end up dead with his face in a table of shit? *He should have been right behind me. He's never deviated from a plan. What had happened*, he thought.

Cracker Jack woke up behind the wheel of the van in an empty parking lot. *Shit, I have got to get back to the warehouse.* He started up the van and headed back to the warehouse. He wasn't sure how he was going to clean this mess up.

So far, he was in the clear, only one person knew about him, and he knew she wouldn't say anything because it would incriminate her. *I'll kill them both, the daughter is halfway dead anyway, and Stump won't be a problem, she won't be missed. Do them both and leave their nude bodies right there. I'll get rid of the goods later. The van doesn't have any windows so I shouldn't have any problems with that.*

Chapter 33

POUND FOR POUND

Ty and JC road back to Ty's place in silence. Once they pulled into the driveway, Ty asked JC to come in for a nightcap before going home. JC was somewhat hesitant to agree but just said, "Sure."

The two men took their drinks to the back patio. As they looked out at the basketball court, pool, trees, and night stars, Ty said, "Remember when we…." That conversation went on for an hour; by drink three, Ty started talking about their couple of days running up and down the highway to look for his little girl. JC just listened as his best friend shared his future uncertainties about his life, daughter, and ex-wife. Once Ty passed out; JC decided to help him to his bedroom before leaving.

When the two men arrived at the master bedroom, JC dropped Ty onto his king-size bed and started to remove his clothes. Ty appeared to be subdued, as JC removed his clothes, he assured him he would find his little girl.

Just as JC was placing the sheet over Ty's nude body, Ty reached out, grabbing JC's hand and saying, "Please don't go. I need you to help me through this."

"We've talked about this over the years. It just doesn't seem to be a good idea for any of us," JC replied.

As Ty was begging please, he removed the sheet to expose his nude body and large pipe. JC just stared, blinking several times and replied with, "Brother, we can't." Ty got up and straddled JC from behind and grabbed his dick and stroked it up and down left to right of JC's back. Ty put his hand inside of JC's pants and stroked his penis, as it thickened, kissing JC along his neck and nibbling on his ear.

As hard as JC tried not to give in, he did. JC became unhinged. He stood and removed his clothes as quickly as he could. He pulled Ty to the end of the bed, bent him over, and jammed his penis into his anus. Ty grabbed his penis and stroked his pipe as JC thrust his penis in and out of his space.

Chapter 34

I'M JUST SAYING

JC grabbed Ty's hips and started moving in and out faster and faster as he begged Ty to take him to a place only the two of them shared. As both men shared the flow of emotion yelling at the top of their lungs "Yes!" JC begged Ty to promise he'll always be his bitch. After a few seconds, they both collapsed as they gasped for air.

JC stayed until morning.

The two men lay in one another's arms as the sun shined in from the dome above the bed. JC said, "Why didn't you tell me the truth about you and Terri's separation?"

Ty sat up and put a pillow behind his back. As he leaned back, he took a deep breath and said, "I'm not sure I should share this with you."

JC replied, "What do you mean? We've always been able to talk, I thought. Until this Terri thing."

Ty suggested JC forget about him and the "Terri thing."
"Now what?"

"Here we are back to where we've been for years. Not being able to let the world know how we feel about each other."

"I'm still with Rae," JC snapped.

"I wasn't sure how you still felt about us until last night."

JC replied with his index finger twirling in the air, "get to the point."

"There's something about Rae…I think you should know. Well, she isn't who you think she is." JC interrupted as he rose and placed his head in the palm of his hand on his elbow, to get a little higher to look Ty into his eyes.

"Rae has been involved with another woman."

"What the fuck are you talking about?"

"Tycie shared a story with me about Rae that I promised I would never repeat." And JC snapped. "Well, Rae was involved with this woman while in Atlanta Georgia; their relationship was serious."

"And that's to do with what now?"

"We don't have to feel guilty about ourselves."

"That was then and this is now!" JC barked.

"No, baby, it is, in fact, now. That lover was Gloria," Ty replied.

JC sat straight up and said, "Man what in the fuck are you talking about?"

"Tycie has been a friend of Gloria's for years. It just turned out this way."

"Does Rae know you know?" JC asked.

"I'm not even sure if Rae's aware that Tycie knows." JC dropped his head on the headboard and blew out hot air. Ty turned toward JC and started teasing his balls while whispering in his ear, "Fuck me" over and over until JC playfully pushed his hand away.

Smiling from ear to ear, JC attempted to say, "Suck my dick bitch—" when Ty stuck his tongue in between his hot soft lips before he could finish his sentence. They enjoyed one another's warm tongues as they both went as deep down one another's throats as they could. Ty reached for JC's hard rock, and decided, *no, that piece of meat needs to be inside of me.* He straggled JC and slowly lowered his buttocks onto JC's thick hard rock.

Ty slowly went up and down on JC's penis inside of his ass as he was saying, "Let's just enjoy each other right now. It's been too long." As Ty worked his magic entertaining JC's pulsating pipe, Ty moved up and down faster and faster as he grabbed his penis and stroked it at the same pace. Both men exploded as they went stiff and collapsed into one another's arms.

Both dicks just dripped as the satisfaction took hold of them both and they drifted off to sleep, with their dicks dripping.

Chapter 35

THE AGREEMENT

Cracker Jack grabbed his cell phone and hit several numbers. The raspy voice said, "What! Where are you? Why has this shit fallen apart?" Cracker Jack suggested she calm down. She asked, "Who's body did you leave at my daughter's house, shit for brains?"

Cracker Jack said, "Body, what in the fuck are you talking about? I went in and did exactly what we agreed on."

"What we agreed on," Terri said, "was that you, not you and others would just scare her and ransack the house. When I heard about the body that was found at my daughter's table facedown in a table of shit, I thought it was you."

"You wish," Cracker Jack said. You're not going to get rid of me that easily. You owe me."

Terri snapped, "I don't owe you shit, this is way out of control, murder wasn't part of the deal."

"Right, but, fucking up your daughter was. News flash, the deal has changed. If you don't give me what you promised, not only will there be one murder, let's not make it two, and I will make sure it all leads right back to you. So, before you do anything you'll regret, take the rest of the night to think about it. Oh, by the way, *She* is aware. You'll hear from me," and before he hung up, he said, "Maybe you should check out the news in North Carolina. You have bigger problems than me. You really should check it out before you fuck with me. Just saying." *Click!*

Terri sat there staring at the screen of a dead phone. Terri refused to believe that She would do this to her. *She wouldn't do this to me, I refuse to believe that.* Terri blurted out, "No one will ruin this! I've come too far to stop now! This delusional psycho has fucked up the plan." *Right now, it doesn't seem like anything leads to me.* As she pondered on that thought, she realized she didn't ask shit for brains about the tracker on the car. That's the only thing that can tie her to this. She had to try and reach out to that psycho again.

How bad is this debacle? Will he answer the phone? The answer to that question is important. I need a full perspective on what the fuck went down.

Chapter 36

BAMBOOZLED

When Rae pulled into their driveway, she wondered why the house was dark. She assumed JC would have kept the lights on until she got home as usual. As she walked toward the front door, the sensors along the walkway picked up the motion and shined light on the front of the house.

Rae went through the front door calling out for JC no response. She went upstairs to their bedroom, bed still made up and no sign of JC. She sat on the edge of the bed confused. She went over the conversation she had with JC before he left to drop Ty off. He assured her he'd see her at home, told her to be careful and gave her a peck on the lips.

Did I misunderstand something? she pondered. *JC and I have never had a problem communicating.*

It was late, Rae decided to take a shower and try and get some sleep. It had been a long couple of days.

At 3:00 p.m. in the afternoon, Rae sat straight up in the bed and looked to her right, no JC. She grabbed her cell phone from the nightstand, no missed calls nor text messages. *What is going on with JC?*

Rae jumped out of bed, yelling, "What in the fuck is going on!" Rae made call after call to JC's cell, only to go to voicemail, and text messages went unanswered. *Oh my God, I pray he's okay! This is not like him.*

Rae attempted to reach Terri, no answer; it went to voicemail. Rae decided to get dressed and go over to Terri's. *Hopefully, she knows something.*

When Rae arrived at Terri's, it was several minutes before Gloria answered the door. Rae stepped in yelling, "What in the fuck is going on? What took you so long to answer the door?"

Gloria looked baffled, and finally said, "Rae, what are you talking about?"

Rae looked at Gloria and said, "Don't fuck with me, Gloria."

"What is this about? What is your problem Rae?"

"Where is Terri? I need to speak with her."

Gloria, responded, "Terri wasn't here when KK and I came down for coffee."

"What do you mean Terri isn't here, Gloria?"

"Like I said, Terri wasn't around when KK and I came downstairs this morning for coffee. And when we went to her bedroom to check on her, her bed was undisturbed."

"Where in the fuck is she, Gloria?" Rae snapped.

"How should I know? However, I will say KK and I were both shocked Terri wasn't here. I don't think she ever went to bed."

"Gloria, what is this all about?" Rae blurted. "JC didn't come home last night. He's not answering his phone or replying to text messages."

Gloria stood there for a few seconds before saying, "Is this unusual?"

Rae shot back, "Yes, it's unusual!"

Gloria suggested Rae have a seat and calm down. As they approached the family space, KK walked in saying, "Is everything okay?"

"Rae seems to have had the same experience you and I had this morning looking for Terri. JC hasn't been seen since last evening."

KK said, "Oh my God, I pray everything is okay." And Gloria agreed.

After a few minutes, Rae said, "Something doesn't seem right. I can't explain what it is, but something's wrong; this situation doesn't feel right."

What in the fuck is up...?

Chapter 37

THIS AND THAT, THAT AND THIS

JC got up to use the bathroom and looked at his cell, where he saw all the missed calls and text messages from Rae. *Oh shit, I've been caught up in the moment.* Ty woke as JC was standing at the foot of the bed seeming confused.

Ty asked, "JC, are you okay?"

JC turned with tears in his eyes saying, "This shouldn't have happened."

"What do you mean, what's going on!" Ty asked.

"Rae has called and texted me within the last several hours. Do you see what time it is? What do I tell her, how do I justify this?"

"Baby, please come here and sit down. We can put all of this into perspective. Let's settle down and talk about this."

"What is there to talk about?" JC asked.

"Have you forgotten what I've told you about Rae and Gloria?" Ty asked.

JC said, "Fuck, two wrongs don't make shit right."

"I understand that; You're missing my point," Ty said.

"And that would be what?" JC asked.

"Now we have leverage. You go home and tell Rae the truth. I'm single, so I don't have to explain myself to anybody. JC, it's time, we have no reason to keep this a secret."

"So, I just walk out on Rae?" JC asked.

Ty grabbed JC's penis aggressively, and said, "Do you love me or not?"

JC flinched and stiffened, saying, "You know I have always loved you."

"Okay, then, it's settled," Ty said. "You go home and give Rae the good news. Just as she freaks out, just say, 'and what about you and Gloria!' 'It's not like you've never been in this situation. You of all people should understand. I'm sorry, I've been living a lie and I can't do it anymore.' That should put her on the defense. And at that point it should be downhill, the two of you should understand one another at that point."

JC casually asked about Terri. "Terri and I parted ways a long time ago. I have no responsibility to no one, other than Tycie!"

"Dude," JC said, "we still haven't found Tycie!"

"What does our relationship have to do with finding Tycie?" Ty asked. "I would hope we continue to pursue that. We must fine her, and I believe you're the one who will. I love you, JC, we can do this, together."

After a few moments, JC agreed, "It's time!" He added, "I must head home before I do anything else. Don't get me wrong, that's the least I can do. Rae has been by my side since I've known her!"

"Brother, you go home and handle your business, you know where to find me." Ty said.

JC replied, "Don't worry, I got this…."

Chapter 38

I'M NOT REALLY IMPRESSED WITH PEOPLE, I'M IMPRESSED WITH RESULTS

Terri used the garage door opener to pull into the garage, jumped out of her car, and blew through the door off from the garage into the house. When Terri walked into the living room, She was standing at the fireplace with a drink in her hand.

As Terri entered the living room, she yelled at the top of her lungs as usual, "Your fucking psycho fucked up the plan. This is not what we agreed to. He's done everything half-ass backwards. He was to follow her home, smack her around a bit, and rob her. Not this bullshit. My daughter is missing, and a dead body was found in her house. How many fucking people are involved? We hired him, not a goddamn football team! His screw-up may have incriminated us as well. And what's this shit about North Carolina!" she shouted.

She did not face Terri, but after a few moments, She coolly said, "Are you done?"

Terri screamed, "Yes!"

She said, "Then sit your motherfucking ass down and shut the fuck up!"

Terri reluctantly sat in the chair to the right of the fireplace. "Cracker Jack, aka psycho, as you call him, has kept me in the know."

"What does that mean?"

"I approved of his actions before his dumbass did anything. So, I have been in the know. Now, let's talk about what you need to know. Should North Carolina be a concern? Maybe not, it depends on the severity of the situation, don't know yet. Now, put that on the backburner until another time. Shit was happening behind the scenes, and decisions had to be made along the way to work through a bad situation. Now we're all in this together, including the football team. So, with that all being in the open, I'm ready to go to bed. Since you're here, it's late. Please don't say another word. What I really need you to do, is to go upstairs and this debacle will be handled tomorrow."

Terri stood, attempting to say, "I can't stay because—"

And She cut her off, by saying, "I'll see you upstairs!" Terri stepped away without another word.

She stood in the doorway of the bedroom enjoying the fragrance of the candles, while staring at Terri on the large bed as she masturbated. Terri slowly rubbed her clitoris, as she started to softly moan. She started removing her clothes as She walked across the room and slowly lay on top of Terri. She sucked on her neck left to right. As She used her tongue to travel between Terri's cleavage and pause at her navel and kissed it. She continued to move toward her pubic hair. She enjoyed rubbing her nose left to right against Terri's soft damp hair. She moved her warm tongue, touched Terri's clitoris. She realized how hard and wet Terri's pussy was. After She ate as much as she could, She lay her body between Terri's legs and the tip of their clitoris touched and within seconds they both exploded pleading with one another not to stop.

Their love making went on for about an hour that seem like days to Terri. They were very compassionate as they pretended to be in love.

Terri eased out of the bed as She slept and stumbled her way to her car. Terri had to get home; she knew Gloria and KK would be looking for her. *Oh my God, I must fix this. I didn't agree to all this bullshit. God has brought me too far to fail me now!*

THE LOST SOUL

As the wind blows you find yourself chasing your soul

As your spirit travels through life there are times you feel alone

Our decisions move us forward because our life story must be told

We all try not to waste our time as we lie pretending to be whole

Who cares about restoring an old lost soul

We see what we want to see as the rest of the world leaves
us standing alone

We should all grab hold of our hearts and not let sin
destroy our soul

Be bold grab your soul and take control

Let common sense be your gift as you grow

No I'm not talking about gold

I'm talking about the lost soul

Diane R.J. Bibbins

If you don't know where you've been, you surely have no clue where you're going. Being born doesn't mean the world owes you anything. How you choose to travel your journey through life will determine your blessings and your destiny, and that is something you're in control of. When you make decisions, you have no one to blame for the outcome but yourself.

I've used realistic life experiences, integrated with fiction, to tell my story.

EPILOGUE

Selina Spaulding aka **Terri,** almost given away at birth, saved by her aunt, **Penny**, despised by her mother, **Angela**, and molested by her father, **Jeff,** growing up. Her mother, **Angela**, hated the child as if it were her fault for being born. Living in the house with them became a challenge to overcome day by day. The child finds herself in a tangled web of deception, deceit, and molestation by her father Jeff. Her life growing up in that environment had been nothing but abuse, neglect, and sexual assault by her father and somehow, she survived. Today she doesn't have that motivation.

I'm sure that bastard **Tyrone Spaulding** aka **Ty** has been molesting our daughter **Tycie Spaulding** for years. He has always controlled her. He managed to turn her against me she whaled. That horrible experience will not happen again, not in my house on my watch!

Selina knew all the tricks associated with molestation such as guilt, shame, and the weakness that follows. The predator makes you feel your only survival is in their hands. Incest is a son of a bitch.

She and Selina met several years ago. The relationship went from lust, sex, to why Terri was available. **She** listened to Terri's life story; it was devastating. She made a promise to Terri. I will rid you of this sin. And to date **She** had kept that promise. "No one will ever fuck you over again. I got you, baby; I promise you that!" **She** kept that promise to date.

Terri nervously, drove home. She came up with a plan, if **Gloria** and **KK** have a problem with this, they can leave. She didn't want them there anyway, now **Rae** may be a bit more of a challenge to get rid of. She decided to address that issue later. They'll all pay, sons of bitches. Unyielding, **Terri** goes into "I don't give a fuck" mode. Saying over and over, *God has brought me too far to fail me now!*

Shout-out to my Family

From left to right: Myself, Ally, Butch, Mommie, Karen and Nana.

Wait! There's more. I would like to give a special shout-out to our brothers, Shawn, and Michael. Unfortunately, the two of them were out of town at the time the above family picture was taken.

My family and I enjoy coming together, praying together, eating together, crying together and most importantly sharing our love together.

I love them all!

   – The Author

CPSIA information can be obtained
at www.ICGtesting.com
Printed in the USA
LVHW011609150922
728475LV00014B/1269

9 781685 372309